KILLER'S WEDGE

ED MCBAIN

Center Point Publishing — *Thorndike, Maine, USA*
Compass Press — *Great Britain and Australia*

First published in 1959 by Simon & Schuster Ltd

Compass Press Large Print Book Series; an imprint of
ISIS Publishing Ltd, Great Britain, and Bolinda Press, Australia
Published in Large Print 2000 by ISIS Publishing Ltd,
7 Centremead, Osney Mead, Oxford, OX2 OES,
Bolinda Publishing Pty Ltd, 17 Mohr Street, Tullamarine, Victoria
3043, Australia by arrangement with Allison & Busby Ltd and
Center Point Publishing, Thorndike, Maine, USA, by arrangement
with Hui Corporation

British Library Cataloguing in Publication Data
McBain, Ed, 1926-
    Killers wedge. – Large print ed.
    1.87th Precinct (Imaginary place) – Fiction 2. Detective and
mystery stories 3. Large type books
    I. Title
    813.5'4[F]

Australian Cataloguing in Publication Data
Killers wedge/ Ed McBain. (Compass Press large print book series)
    1. Large print books 2. 87th Precinct (Imaginary place) – Fiction
    3. City and town life – Fiction 4. Police – Fiction
    5. Detective and mystery stories, American
    I. Title
    813.54

Library of Congress Cataloguing in Publication Data
McBain, Ed., 1926-
    Killer's wedge / Ed McBain.
    p. cm.
    [ISBN 1-58547-032-5 (lib. bdg, : alk paper)]
    1. 87th Precinct (Imaginary Place) – Fiction. 2. City and town
life – Fiction 3. Police – Fiction 4. Large type books I. Title

ISBN 0-7531-6138-9 (hb) ISBN 0-7531-6338-1 (pb)
(Isis Publishing Ltd)
ISBN 1-74030-184-6 (hb) ISBN 1-74030-185-4 (pb)
(Bolinda Publishing Pty Ltd)
ISBN 1-58547-032-5 (hb)
(Center Point Publishing)

Printed and bound by Antony Rowe, Chippenham and Reading

This is for
HELEN and GENE

The city in these pages is imaginary.
The people, the places are all fictitious.
Only the police routine is based on established
investigatory technique

CHAPTER
ONE

It was a normal everyday afternoon at the beginning of October.

Outside the grilled windows of the 87th's squadroom, Grover Park was aflame with color. Indian summer, like a Choctaw princess, strutted her feathers, wiggled her bright reds and oranges and yellows on the mild October air. The sun was dazzling in a flawlessly blue sky, its rays pushing at the grilled windows, creating shafts of golden light which dust motes tirelessly climbed. The sounds of the street outside slithered over the window sills and through the open windows, joining with the sounds of the squadroom to create a melody unique and somehow satisfying.

Like a well-constructed symphony, there was an immediately identifiable theme to the sounds inside the squadroom. This theme was built on a three-part harmony of telephone rings, typewriter clackings, and profanities. Upon this theme, the symphony was pyramided into its many variations. The variations ranged from the splendid *wooshy* sound of a bull's fist crashing into a thief's belly, to the shouted roar of a bull wanting to know where the hell his ball-point-pen had gone, to the quietly persistent verbal bludgeoning of an interrogation session, to the muted honey tones of a phone conversation with a Hall Avenue debutante, to the whistling of a rookie delivering a message from Headquarters, to the romantic bellow of a woman filing a complaint against her wife-beating husband, to the gurgle of the water cooler, to the uninhibited laughter following a dirty story.

Such laughter, accompanied by the outside street sounds of October, greeted the punch line of Meyer Meyer's joke on that Friday afternoon.

"He really knows how to tell them," Bert Kling said. "That's the one thing I can't do. Tell a story."

"There are *many* things you can't do," Meyer answered, his blue eyes twinkling, "but we'll excuse the slight inaccuracy. Storytelling, Bert, is an art acquired with age. A young snot like you could never hope to tell a good story. It takes years and years of experience."

"Go to hell, you old fart," Kling said.

"Right away he gets aggressive, you notice that, Cotton? He's very sensitive about his age."

Cotton Hawes sipped at his coffee and grinned. He was a tall man, six feet two and weighing in at a hundred and ninety pounds. He had blue eyes and a square jaw with a cleft chin. His hair was a brilliant red, lighted now by the lazy October sunshine which played with particular intensity on the streak of white hair over his left temple. The white streak was a curiosity in that it was the result of a long-ago knife wound. They'd shaved the original red to get at the cut, and the shaved patch had grown in white. "Which shows how goddamn scared I was," Hawes had said at the time.

2

Now, grinning at Meyer, he said, "The very young are always hostile. Didn't you know that?"

"Are *you* starting on me, too?" Kling said. "It's a conspiracy."

"It's not a conspiracy," Meyer corrected. "It's a spontaneous program of hatred. That's the trouble with this world. Too much hatred. By the way, do either of you know the slogan for Anti-Hate Week?"

"No," Hawes said in a perfect straight-man voice. "What is the slogan for Anti-Hate Week?"

"Screw-All-Haters!" Meyer said vehemently, and the phone rang. Hawes and Kling looked puzzled for a moment, and then burst into belated laughter. Meyer shushed them with an outstretched palm.

"Eighty-seventh Squad, Detective Meyer speaking," he said. "What was that, ma'am? Yes, I'm a detective. What? Well, no, I'm not exactly in charge of the squad." He shrugged and raised his eyebrows in Kling's direction.

"Well, the lieutenant is pretty busy right now. May I help you, ma'am? Yes, ma'am, what is it? A bitch, you say? Yes, ma'am. I see. Well, ma'am, we can't very well keep him at home. That is not exactly the job of the police department. I understand. The bitch . . . Yes, ma'am. Well, we can't spare a man right now. We're a little short this afternoon . . . What? . . . Well, I'm sorry you feel that way. But you see . . ."

He stopped and stared at the receiver.

"She hung up," he said, and replaced the phone on its cradle.

"What was that all about?" Kling asked

3

"She's got a great Dane who keeps chasing after this cocker spaniel bitch. She wants us to either keep the great Dane home or do something about the bitch." Meyer shrugged again. "*L'amour, l'amour*. Always troubles with *l'amour*." He paused. "You know what love is?"

"No, what's love?" Hawes said, straight-manning it again.

"I'm not joking this time," Meyer said. "I'm philosophizing. Love is only low-key hate."

"Christ, what a cynic!" Hawes said.

"I'm not cynical, I'm philosophizing. And you should never believe a man when he's thinking out loud. How else can he test brilliant ideas unless he voices them?"

Hawes turned suddenly.

The woman who stood just outside the slatted-rail divider which separated the squadroom from the corridor had entered so silently that none of the men had heard her approach. She had just cleared her throat, and the sound was shockingly loud, so that Kling and Meyer turned to face her at almost the same moment Hawes did.

She looked for a moment like Death personified.

She had deep black hair pulled into a bun at the back of her head. She had brown eyes set in a face without makeup, without lipstick, a face so chalky white that it seemed she had just come from a sickbed somewhere. She wore a black overcoat and black shoes with no stockings. Her bare legs were as white as her face, thin legs which seemed incapable of supporting her. She

4

carried a large black tote bag, and she clung to the black leather handles with thin bony fingers.

"Yes?" Hawes said.

"Is Detective Carella here?" she asked. Her voice was toneless.

"No," Hawes said. "I'm Detective Hawes. May I hel —"

"When will he be back?" she interrupted.

"That's difficult to say. He had something personal to take care of, and then he was going directly to an outside assignment. Perhaps one of us —"

"I'll wait," the woman said.

"It may take quite a while."

"I have all the time in the world," she answered.

Hawes shrugged. "Well, all right. There's a bench outside. If you'll just —"

"I'll wait inside," she said, and before Hawes could stop her she had pushed open the gate in the railing and started walking toward one of the empty desks in the center of the room. Hawes started after her immediately.

"Miss, I'm sorry," he said, "but visitors are not permitted —"

"*Mrs.*," she corrected. "Mrs. Frank Dodge." She sat. She placed the heavy black bag on her lap, both hands resting firmly on its open top."

"Well, Mrs. Dodge, we don't allow visitors inside the squadroom except on business. I'm sure you can appreciate —"

"I'm here on business," she said. She pressed her unpainted lips together into a thin line.

"Well then, can you tell me . . . ?"

"I'm waiting for Detective Carella," she said. "Detective Steve Carella," and she said the last words with surprising bitterness.

"If you're waiting for him," Hawes said patiently, "you'll have to wait on the bench outside. I'm sorry, but that's —"

"I'll wait right here," she said firmly. "And you'll wait, too."

Hawes glanced at Meyer and Kling.

"Lady," Meyer started, "we don't want to seem rude . . ."

"Shut up!" the woman said.

There was the unmistakable ring of command in her voice. The detectives stared at her.

Her hand slipped into the pocket on the right-hand side of her coat. When it emerged, it was holding something cold and hard.

"This is a .38," the woman said.

CHAPTER
TWO

The woman with the .38 and the black tote bag sat motionless in the straight-backed wooden chair. The street noises outside the squadroom seemed to magnify the silence that had followed her simple declaration. The three detectives looked first at each other and then back to the woman and the unwavering .38.

"Give me your guns," she said.

The detectives did not move.

"Give me your guns, or I'll fire."

"Look, lady," Meyer said, "put up the piece. We're all friends here. You're only going to get yourself in trouble."

"I don't care," she said. "Put your guns on the desk here in front of me. Don't try to take them out of the holsters or I'll shoot. This gun is pointed right at the redheaded one's belly. Now move!"

Again, the detectives hesitated.

"All right, redhead," she said. "Say your prayers."

There was not a man in that room who did not realize that once he relinquished his weapon he would be at the mercy of the woman holding the gun. There was not a man in that room, too, who had not faced a gun at one time or another in his career. The men in that room were cops, but they were also human beings who did not particularly relish the thought of an early grave. The men in that room were human beings, but they were also cops who knew the destructive power of a .38, who also knew that women were as capable of squeezing triggers as were men, who realized that this woman holding the gun could cut down all three of them in one hasty volley. And yet, they hesitated.

"Damnit!" she shouted. "I'm not kidding!"

Kling was the first to move, and then only because he saw the knuckle-white tension of the woman's trigger finger. Staring at her all the while, he unstrapped his shoulder rig and dropped holster and Police Special to the desk top. Meyer unclipped his holster from his right hip pocket and deposited it alongside Kling's gun. Hawes carried his .38 just off his right hipbone. He unclipped the holster and put it on the desk.

"Which of these desk drawers lock?" the woman asked.

"The top one," Hawes said.

"Where's the key?"

"In the drawer."

She opened the drawer, found the key, and then shoved the guns into the drawer. She locked the desk then, removed the key, and put it into her coat pocket. The big black purse was still on her lap.

"Okay, now you got our guns," Meyer said. "Now what? What is this, lady?"

"I'm going to kill Steve Carella," the woman said.

"Why?"

"Never mind why. Who else is in this place right now?"

8

Meyer hesitated. From where the woman was sitting, she had a clear view of both the lieutenant's office and the corridor outside the squadroom . . .

"Answer me!" she snapped.

"Just Lieutenant Byrnes," Meyer lied In the Clerical Office, just outside the slatted-rail divider, Miscolo was busily working on his records. There was the possibility that they could maneuver her so that her back was to the corridor. And then, if Miscolo decided to enter the squad room on one of his frequent trips, perhaps he would grasp the situation and . . .

"Get the lieutenant," she said.

Meyer began to move.

"Before you go, remember this. The gun is on you. One phony move, and I shoot. And I keep shooting until every man in this place is dead. Now go ahead. Knock on the lieutenant's door and tell him to get out here."

Meyer crossed the silent squadroom. The lieutenant's door was closed. He rapped on the wooden frame alongside the frosted glass.

"Come!" Byrnes called from behind the door.

"Pete, it's me. Meyer."

"The door's unlocked," Byrnes answered.

"Pete, you better come out here."

"What the hell is it?"

"Come on out, Pete."

There was the sound of footsteps behind the door. The door opened. Lieutenant Peter Byrnes, as compact as a rivet, thrust his muscular neck and shoulders into the opening.

"What is it, Meyer? I'm busy."

"There's a woman wants to see you."

"A woman? Where . . . ?" His eyes flicked past Meyer to where the woman sat. Instant recognition crossed his face. "Hello, Virginia," he said, and then he saw the gun.

"Get in here, Lieutenant," Virginia Dodge said.

A frown had come over Byrnes' face. His brows pulled down tightly over scrutinizing blue eyes. Intelligence flashed on his craggy face. Lumberingly, like a man about to lift a heavy log, he crossed the squadroom, walking directly to where Virginia Dodge sat. He seemed ready to pick her up and hurl her into the corridor.

"What is this, Virginia?" he said, and there was the tone of a father in his voice, a rather angry father speaking to a fifteen-year-old daughter who'd come home too late after a dance.

"What does it look like, Lieutenant?"

"It looks like you've blown your wig, that's what it looks like. What the hell's the gun for? What are you doing in here with . . ."

"I'm going to kill Steve Carella," Virginia said.

"Oh, for Christ's sake," Byrnes said in exasperation. "Do you think that's going to help your husband any?"

"Nothing's going to help Frank any more."

"What do you mean?"

"Frank died yesterday. In the hospital at Castleview Prison."

Byrnes was silently meditative. He did not speak for a long while, and then he said only, "You can't blame Carella for that."

"Carella sent him up."

10

"Your husband was a criminal."

"Carella sent him up."

"Carella only arrested him. You can't —"

"*And* pressed the D.A. for a conviction, *and* testified at the trial *and* did everything in his power to make sure Frank went to jail!"

"Virginia, he —"

"Frank was sick! Carella knew that! He knew that when he put him away!"

"Virginia, for Christ's sake, our job is to —"

"Carella killed him as sure as if he'd shot him. And now I'm going to kill Carella. The minute he steps into this squadroom, I'm going to kill him."

"And then what? How do you expect to get out of here, Virginia? You haven't got a chance."

Virginia smiled thinly. "I'll get out, all right."

"Will you? You fire a gun in here, and every cop in ten miles will come barging upstairs."

"I'm not worried about that, Lieutenant."

"No, huh? Talk sense, Virginia. You want to get the electric chair? Is that what you want?"

"I don't care. I don't want to live without Frank."

Byrnes paused for a long time. Then he said, "I don't believe you, Virginia."

"What don't you believe? That I'm going to kill Carella? That I'll shoot the first one who does anything to stop me?"

"I don't believe you're fool enough to use that gun. I'm walking out of here, Virginia. I'm walking back to my office . . ."

"No, you're not!"

"Yes, I am. I'm walking back to my office, and here's why. There are four men in this room, counting me. You can shoot me, maybe, and maybe another one after me . . . but you'll have to be pretty fast and pretty accurate to get all of us."

"I'll get all of you, Lieutenant," Virginia said, and the thin smile reappeared on her mouth.

"Yeah, well I'm not willing to bet on that. Jump her the minute she fires, men." He paused. "I'm going to my office, Virginia, and I'm going to sit in there for five minutes. When I come out, you'd better be gone, and we'll forget all about this. Otherwise I'm going to slap you silly and take that gun away from you and dump you into the detention cells downstairs. Now is that clear, Virginia?"

"It's very clear."

"Five minutes," Byrnes said curtly, and he wheeled and started toward his office.

With supreme confidence in her voice, Virginia said, "I don't have to shoot you, Lieutenant."

Byrnes did not break his stride.

"I don't have to shoot *any* of you."

He continued walking.

"I've got a bottle of nitroglycerin in my purse."

Her words came like an explosion. Byrnes stopped in his tracks and turned slowly to face her, his eyes dropping to the big black bag in her lap. She had turned the barrel of me gun so that it pointed at the bag now, so that its muzzle was thrust into the opening at the top of the bag.

12

"I don't believe you, Virginia," Byrnes said, and he turned and reached for the doorknob again.

"Don't open that door, Lieutenant," Virginia shouted, "or I'll fire into this purse and we can *all* go to Hell!"

He thought in that moment before twisting the doorknob, *She's lying. She hasn't got any soup in that purse, where would she get any?*

And then he remembered that among her husband's many criminal offences had been a conviction for safe-blowing.

But she hasn't any soup, he thought, *Jesus, that's crazy. But suppose she does? But she won't explode it. She's waiting for Carella. She wouldn't . . .*

And then he thought simply, *Meyer Meyer has a wife and three children.*

Slowly, he let his hand drop. Wearily, he turned to Virginia Dodge.

"That's better," she said. "Now let's wait for Carella."

Steve Carella was nervous.

Sitting alongside Teddy, his wife, he could feel nervousness ticking along the backs of his hands, twitching in his fingers. Clean-shaved, his high cheekbones and downward-slanting eyes giving him an almost Oriental appearance, he sat with his mouth tensed, and the doctor smiled gently.

"Well, Mr. Carella," Dr. Randolph said, "your wife is going to have a baby."

The nervousness fled almost instantly. The cork had been pulled, and the violent waters of his tension over-ran the tenuous walls of the dike, leaving only the muddy silt of uncertainty. If anything, the uncertainty was worse. He hoped it did not show. He did not want it to show to Teddy.

"Mr. Carella," the doctor said, "I can see the prenatal jitters erupting all over you. Relax. There's nothing to worry about."

Carella nodded, but even the nod lacked conviction. He could feel the presence of Teddy beside him, his Teddy, his Theodora, the girl he loved, the woman he'd married. He turned for an instant to look at her face, framed with hair as black as midnight, the brown eyes gleaming with pride now, the silent red lips slightly parted.

I mustn't spoil it for her, he thought.

And yet he could not shake the doubt.

"May I reassure you on several points, Mr. Carella?" Randolph said.

"Well, I really . . ."

"Perhaps you're worried about the infant. Perhaps, because your wife is a deaf mute, born that way . . . perhaps you feel the infant may also be born handicapped. This is a reasonable fear, Mr. Carella."

"I . . ."

"But a completely unfounded one," Randolph smiled. "Medicine is in many respects a cistern of ignorance — but we *do* know that deafness, though sometimes congenital, is not hereditary. For example, perfectly normal offspring have been produced by *two* deaf parents. Lon Chaney is the most famous of these offspring, I suppose. With the proper care and treatment, your wife will go through a normal pregnancy and

14

deliver a normal baby. She's a healthy animal, Mr. Carella. And if I may be so bold, a very beautiful one."

Teddy Carella, reading the doctor's lips, came close to blushing. Her beauty, like a rare rose garden which a horticulturist has come to take for granted, was a thing she'd accepted for a long time now. It always came as a surprise, therefore, when someone referred to it in glowing terms. These were the face and the body with which she had been living for a good many years. She could not have been less concerned over whether or not they pleased the strangers of the world. She wanted them to please one person alone: Steve Carella. Now, with Steve's acceptance of the idea coupling with her own thrilled anticipation, she felt a soaring sense of joy.

"Thank you, Doctor," Carella said.

"Not at all," Randolph answered. "Good luck to you both. I'll want to see you in a few weeks, Mrs. Carella. Now take care of her."

"I will," Carella answered, and they left the obstetrician's office. In the corridor outside, Teddy threw herself into his arms and kissed him violently.

"Hey!" he said. "Is that any way for a pregnant woman to behave?"

Teddy nodded, her eyes glowing mischievously. With one sharp twist of her dark head, she gestured toward the elevators.

"You want to go home, huh?"

She nodded.

"And then what?"

Teddy Carella was eloquently silent.

"It'll have to wait," he said. "There's a little suicide I'm supposed to be covering."

He pressed the button for the elevator.

"I behaved like a jerk, didn't I?"

Teddy shook her head.

"I did. I was worried. About you, and about the baby . . ." He paused. "But I've got an idea. First of all, to show my appreciation for the most wonderfully fertile and productive wife in the city . . ."

Teddy grinned.

". . . I would like us both to have a drink. We'll drink to you and the baby, darling." He took her into his arms. "You because I love you so much. And the baby because he s going to share our love." He kissed the tip of her nose. "And then off to my suicide. But is that all? Not by a longshot. This is a day to remember. This is the day the most beautiful woman in the United States, nope, the world, hell, the universe, discovered she was going to have a baby! So . . ." He looked at his watch. "I should be back at the squadroom by about seven latest. Will you meet me there? I'll have to do a report, and then we'll go out to dinner, some quiet place where I can hold your hand and lean over to kiss you whenever I want to. Okay? At seven?"

Teddy nodded happily.

"And then home. And then . . . is it decent to make love to a pregnant woman?"

Teddy nodded emphatically, indicating that it was not only decent but perfectly acceptable and moral and absolutely necessary.

"I love you," Carella said gruffly. "Do you know that?"

16

She knew it. She did not say a word. She would not have said a word even if she could have. She looked at him, and her eyes were moist, and he said, "I love you more than life."

CHAPTER
THREE

There were ninety-thousand people living in the 87th Precinct.

The streets of the precinct ran south from the River Harb to Grover Park, which was across the way from the station house. The River Highway paralleled the river's course, and beyond that was.the first precinct street, fancy Silvermine Road, which still sported elevator operators and doormen in its tall apartment buildings. Continuing south, the precinct ran through the gaudy commercialism of The Stem, and then Ainsley Avenue, and then Culver with its dowdy tenements, its unfrequented churches, and its overflowing bars. Mason Avenue, familiarly known as "La Via de Putas" to the Puerto Ricans, "Whore Street," to the cops, was south of Culver and then came Grover Avenue and the park. The precinct stretch was a short one from north to south. Actually, it extended into Grover Park but only on a basis of professional courtesy; the park territory was officially under the joint command of the neighboring 88th and 89th. The stretch from east to west, however, was a longer one consisting of thirty-five tightly packed side streets. Even so, the entire territory of the precinct did not cover very much ground. It seemed even smaller when considering the vast number of people who lived there.

The immigration pattern of America and, as a consequence, the integration pattern were clearly evident in the streets of the 87th. The population was composed almost entirely of third-generation Irish, Italians, and Jews, and first-generation Puerto Ricans. The immigrant groups did not make the slum. Conversely, it was the slum with its ghetto atmosphere of acceptance which attracted the immigrant groups. The rents, contrary to popular belief, were not low. They were as high as many to be found anywhere else in the city and, considering the services rendered for the money, they were exorbitant. Nonetheless, even a slum can become home. Once settled into it, the inhabitants of the 87th put up pictures on chipped plaster walls, threw down scatter rugs on splintered wooden floors. They learned good American tenement occupations like banging on the radiators for heat, stamping on the cockroaches which skittered across the kitchen floor whenever a light was turned on, setting traps for the mice and rats which paraded through the apartment like the *Wehrmacht* through Poland, adjusting the unbending steel bar of a police lock against the entrance door to the flat.

It was the job of the policemen of the 87th to keep the inhabitants from engaging in another popular form of slum activity: the pursuit of a life of criminal adventure.

Virginia Dodge wanted to know how many men were doing this job.

"We've got sixteen detectives on the squad," Byrnes told her.

"Where are they now?"

"Three are right here."

"And the rest?"

"Some are off duty, some are answering squeals, and some are on plants."

"Which?"

"You want a complete rundown, for Christ's sake?"

"Yes."

"Look, Virginia . . ." The pistol moved a fraction of an inch deeper into the purse. "Okay. Cotton, get the duty chart."

Hawes looked at the woman. "Is it okay to move?" he asked.

"Go ahead. Don't open any desk drawers. Where's *your* gun, Lieutenant?"

"I don't carry one."

"You're lying to me. Where is it? In your office?"

Byrnes hesitated.

"Goddamnit," Virginia shouted, "let's get something straight here! I'm dead serious, and the next person who lies to me, or who doesn't do what I tell him to do when I —"

"All right, all right, take it easy," Byrnes said. "It's in my desk drawer." He turned and started for his office.

"Just a minute," Virginia said. "We'll *all* go with you." She picked up her bag gingerly and then swung her gun at the other men in the room. "Move," she said. "Follow the lieutenant."

Like a small herd of cattle, the men followed Byrnes into the office. Virginia crowded into the small room after them. Byrnes walked to his desk.

20

"Take it out of the drawer and put it on the desk," Virginia said. "Grab it by the muzzle. If your finger comes anywhere near the trigger, the nitro . . ."

"All right, all right," Byrnes said impatiently.

He hefted the revolver by its barrel and placed it on the desk top. Virginia quickly picked up the gun and put it into the left-hand pocket of her coat.

"Outside now," she said.

Again, they filed into the squadroom. Virginia sat at the desk she had taken as her command post. She placed the purse on the desk before her, and then levered the .38 at it. "Get me the duty chart," she said.

"Get it, Cotton," Byrnes said.

Hawes went for the chart. It hung on the wall near one of the rear windows, a simple black rectangle into which white celluloid letters were inserted. It was a detective's responsibility to replace the name of the cop he'd relieved with his own whenever his tour of duty started. Unlike patrolmen, who worked five eight-hour shifts and then swung for the next fifty-six hours, the detectives chose their own duty teams. Since there were sixteen of them attached to the squad, their teams automatically broke down into groups of five, five and five — with a loose man kicking around from shift to shift. On this bright everyday afternoon in October, six detectives were listed on the duty chart. Three of them — Hawes, Kling and Meyer — were in the squadroom.

"Where are the other three?" Virginia asked.

"Carella took his wife to the doctor," Byrnes said.

"How sweet," Virginia said bitterly.

"And then he's got a suicide he's working on."

"When will he be back?"

"I don't know."

"You must have some idea."

"I have no idea. He'll be back when he's ready to come back."

"What about the other two men?"

"Brown's on a plant. The back of a tailor shop."

"A what?"

"A plant. A stakeout, call it what you want to. He's sitting there waiting for the place to be held up."

"Don't kid me, Lieutenant."

"I'm not kidding, damnit. Four tailor shops in the neighborhood have been held up during the daylight hours. We expect this one to get hit soon. Brown's waiting for the thief to show."

"When will he come back to the squadroom?"

"A little after dark, I imagine. Unless the thief hits. What time is it now?" Byrnes looked up at the clock on the wall. "4:38. I imagine he'll be back by six or so."

"And the last one? Willis?"

Byrnes shrugged. "He was here a half-hour ago. Who's catching?"

"I am," Meyer said.

"Well, where'd Willis go?"

"He's out on a squeal, Pete. A knifing on Mason."

"That's where he is then," Byrnes said to Virginia.

"And when will *he* be back?"

"I don't know."

"Soon?"

"I imagine so."

"Who else is in the building?"

22

"The desk sergeant and the desk lieutenant. You passed them on your way in."

"Yes?"

"Captain Frick, who commands the entire precinct in a sense."

"What do you mean?"

"I control the squad, but officially . . ."

"Where's he?"

"His office is downstairs."

"Who else?"

"There are a hundred and eighty-six patrolmen attached to this precinct," Byrnes said. "A third of them are on duty now. Some of them are roaming around the building. The rest are out on their beats."

"What are they doing in the building?"

"Twenty-fours mostly." Byrnes paused and then translated. "Duty as records clerks."

"When does the shift change again?"

"At a quarter to midnight."

"Then they won't be back until then? The ones on beats?"

"Most of them'll be relieved on post. But they usually come back to change into their street clothes before going home."

"Will any detectives be coming up here? Besides the ones listed on the duty chart?"

"Possibly."

"We're not supposed to be relieved until eight in the morning, Pete," Meyer said.

"But Carella will be back long before then, won't he?" Virginia asked.

"Probably."

"Yes or no?"

"I can't say for sure. I'm playing this straight with you, Virginia. Carella may get a lead which'll keep him out of the office. I don't know."

"Will he call in?"

"Maybe."

"If he does, tell him to come right back here. Do you understand?"

"Yes. I understand."

The telephone rang. It cut the conversation and then shrilled persistently into the silence of the squadroom.

"Answer it," Virginia said. "No funny stuff."

Meyer picked up the receiver. "Eighty-seventh Squad." he said, "Detective Meyer speaking." He paused. "Yes, Dave. Go ahead, I'm listening." He was aware all at once of the fact that Virginia Dodge was hearing only one-half of the telephone conversation with the desk sergeant. Casually, patiently, he listened.

"Meyer, we got a call a little while back from some guy who heard shots and a scream from the apartment next to his. I sent a car over, and they just reported back. A dame got shot in the arm, and her boyfriend claims the gun went off accidentally while he was cleaning it. You want to send one of the boys over?"

"Sure, what's the address?" Meyer said, patiently watching Virginia.

"23-79 Culver. That's next door to the Easy Bar. You know it?"

"I know it. Thanks, Dave."

"Okay." Meyer put up the phone. "That was a lady calling," Meyer said. "Dave thought we ought to take it."

24

"Who's Dave?" Virginia asked.

"Murchison. The desk sergeant," Byrnes said. "What is it, Meyer?"

"This lady says somebody's trying to break into her apartment. She wants us to send a detective over right away."

Byrnes and Meyer exchanged a long knowing glance. Such a call would have been handled by the desk sergeant directly, and he would not have annoyed the Detective Division with it. He'd have dispatched a radio motor patrol car immediately.

"Either that or he wants you to contact the captain and see what he can do about it," Meyer said.

"All right, I'll do that," Byrnes said. "Is that all right with you, Virginia?"

"No one's leaving this room," Virginia said.

"I know that. Which is why I'm passing the call on to Captain Frick. Is that all right?"

"Go ahead" she said. "No tricks."

"The address is 23-79 Culver," Meyer said.

"Thanks." Byrnes dialed three numbers and waited. Captain Frick picked up the phone on the second ring.

"Yop?" he said.

"John, this is Pete."

"Oh, hello, Pete. How goes it?"

"So-so. John, I've got a special favor I'd like you to do."

"What's that?"

"Some woman at 23-79 Culver is complaining that someone's trying to get into her apartment. I can't spare a man right now. Could you get a patrolman over there?"

"What?" Frick said.

"I know it's an unusual request. We'd ordinarily handle it ourselves, but we're kind of busy."

"What?" Frick said again.

"Can you do it, John?" Standing with the receiver to his ear, Byrnes watched the shrewdly calculating eyes of Virginia Dodge. *Come on, John*, he thought. *Wake up, for Christ's sake!*

"*You'd* ordinarily handle it?" Frick asked. "Boy, that's a laugh. I've got to kill myself to get you to take a *legitimate* squeal. Why bother me with this, Pete? Why don't you just give it to the desk sergeant?" Frick paused. "How the hell'd you get a hold of it anyway? Who's on the desk?"

"Will you take care of it, John?"

"Are you kidding me, Pete? What is this?" Frick began laughing. "Your joke for today, huh? Okay, I bit. How's everything upstairs?"

Byrnes hesitated for a moment, phrasing his next words carefully. Then, watching Virginia, he said, "Not so hot."

"What's the matter? Headaches?"

"Plenty. Why don't you go up and see for yourself?"

"Up? Up where?"

Come on, Byrnes thought. *Think! For just one lousy minute of your life, think!*

"It's part of your job, isn't it?" Byrnes said.

"What's part of my job? Hey, what's the matter with you, Pete? You flipped or something?"

"Well, I think you ought to find out," Byrnes said.

"Find out *what*? Holy Jesus, you have flipped."

26

"I'll be expecting you to do that then," Byrnes said, aware of a frown starting on Virginia's forehead.

"Do what?"

"Go up there to check on it. Thanks a lot, John."

"You know, I don't understand a damn thing you're —" and Byrnes hung up.

"All settled?" Virginia asked.

"Yes."

She stared at Byrnes thoughtfully. "There are extensions on all these phones, aren't there?" she said.

"Yes," Byrnes said.

"Fine. I'll be listening to any other call that goes in or out of this place."

CHAPTER
FOUR

The problem, Byrnes thought, is that we cannot communicate with each other. This, surely, has been the problem of the human race since the beginning of time, but it's especially aggravated right here and right now. I'm in my own squadroom with three capable detectives, and we can't sit down together to discuss the ways and means of getting that gun and that nitro — if the nitro exists — away from that menacing little bitch. Four intelligent men with a nut cruncher of a problem, and we have no way of talking it out. Not with her sitting there. Not with that .38 in her fist.

And so, lacking communication, I also lack command. In effect, Virginia Dodge now commands the 87th Squad.

She'll continue to command it until one of two things happens:

a) We disarm her.

b) Steve Carella arrives and she shoots him.

There is, of course, a third possibility. There is the possibility that she'll get rattled and put a bullet into that purse with its alleged jar of nitro, and there we go. No more waiting for next week's chapter. It'll all be over in a mighty big way. They will probably hear the blast away the hell over in the 88th. The blast might even knock the commissioner out of bed. Assuming, of course, that there really is a jar of nitro in that bag. Unfortunately, we cannot proceed as if there isn't. We have to assume, along with Virginia Dodge, that the jar of nitro is as real as the .38. In which case, another interesting possibility presents itself. We can't fool around here. We can't go playing grab-ass because nitroglycerine is very potent stuff which can explode on the slightest provocation. Where the hell did she get a jar of nitro? From her safecracker husband's hope chest?

But even safecrackers — except in Scandinavia — don't use it on blow jobs any more. It's too damn unpredictable. I've known safecrackers who, when using nitro, carried it in a hot-water bottle.

So there she sits with a jar full of the stuff in her purse.

I wonder if she rode the subway with it in her purse? Brynes thought, and he smiled grimly.

Okay, the nitro is real. We play it as if it's real. It's the only way we *can* play it. And this means no sudden moves, no grabs for the purse.

So what *do* we do?

Wait for Carella? And what time will he be back? What time is it now?

He looked up at the wall clock. 5:07.

Still broad daylight outside — well, maybe a hint of dusk — but still a golden afternoon, really. Does anyone out there know we're playing footsie with a bottle of soup?

No one, Byrnes thought. Not even meatheaded Captain Frick. How do you set a fire under that man, how do you get the wall of bricks to fall on his head?

How the hell do we get out of this mess?

I wonder if she smokes, Byrnes thought.

If she smokes . . . Now wait a minute . . . now, let's work this out sensibly. Let's say she smokes. Okay. Okay, we've got that much. Now . . . if we can get her to put the purse on the desk, get it off her lap. That shouldn't be too hard . . . Where's the purse now? . . . Still in her lap . . . Virginia Dodge's goddamn lap dog, a bottle of nitro . . . Okay, let's say I can get her to put the purse on the desk, out of the way . . . Then let's say I offer her a cigarette and then start to light it for her.

If I drop the lighted match in her lap, she'll jump a mile.

And when she jumps, I'll hit her.

I'm not worried about that .38 — well, I'm worried, who the hell wants to get shot — but I'm not really worried about it so long as that soup is out of the way. I don't want to have a scuffle anywhere near that explosive. I've faced guns before, but nitro is another thing and I don't want them blotting me off the wall.

I wonder if she smokes.

"How have you been, Virginia?" Byrnes asked.

"You can cut it right now, Lieutenant."

"Cut what?"

"The sweet talk. I didn't come here to listen to any of your crap. I heard enough of that last time I was here."

"That was a long time ago, Virginia."

"Five years, three months, and seventeen days. That's how long ago it was."

"We don't make the laws, Virginia," Byrnes said gently. "We only enforce them. And when a person breaks . . ."

"I don't want a lecture. My husband is dead. Steve Carella sent him up. That's good enough for me."

"Steve only arrested him. A jury tried him, and a judge sentenced him."

"But Carella . . ."

"Virginia, you're forgetting something, aren't you?"

"What?"

"Your husband blinded a man."

"That was an accident."

"Your husband fired a gun at a man during a holdup and deprived that man of his eyesight. And he didn't fire the gun by accident."

"He fired because the man began yelling cop. What would you have done?"

"I wouldn't have been holding up a gas station to begin with."

"No, huh? Big simon-pure Lieutenant Byrnes. I heard all about your junkie son, Lieutenant. The big shot cop with the drug-addict son."

"That was a long time ago, too, Virginia. My son is all right now."

He could never think back to that time in his life without some pain. Oh, not as much as in the beginning, no, there would never again be that much pain for him, the pain of discovering that his only son was a tried-and-true drug addict, hooked through the bag and back again. A drug addict possibly involved in a homicide. Those had been days of black pain for Peter Byrnes, days when he had withheld information from the men of his own squad, until finally he had told everything to Steve Carella. Carella had almost lost his life working on that case. It had been touch and go after he'd been shot, and no man ever had prayed the way Byrnes did for any other man's recovery. But it was all over now, except for the slight twinge of pain whenever he thought of it. The habit had been kicked, the household was in order. And now, Steve Carella, a man Byrnes almost considered as another son, had a rendezvous with a woman in black. And the woman in black spelled death.

"I'm glad your son is all right now," Virginia said sarcastically. "My husband isn't. My husband is dead. And the way I read it, Carella killed him. Now let's cut the crap, shall we?"

"I'd rather talk awhile."

"Then talk to yourself. I'm not interested." Byrnes sat on the corner of the desk. Virginia shifted the purse in her lap, the revolver pointing into the opening. "Don't come any closer, Lieutenant. I'm warning you."

"What are your plans, exactly, Virginia?"

"I've already told you. When Carella gets here, I'm going to kill him. And then I'm going to leave. And if anyone tries to stop me, I drop the bag with the nitro."

"Suppose I try to get that gun away from you right this minute?"

"I wouldn't if I were you."

"Suppose I tried?"

"I'm banking on something, Lieutenant."

"What's that?"

"The fact that no man is really a hero. Whose life is more important to you — yours or Carella's? You make a try for the gun, and there's a chance the nitro will go off in your face. *Your* face, not his. All right, you'll have saved Carella. But you'll have destroyed yourself."

"Carella may mean a lot to me, Virginia. I might be willing to die for him."

"Yeah? And how much does he mean to the other men in this room? Would they be willing to die for him, too? Or for the crumby salary they're getting from the city? Why don't you take a vote, Lieutenant, and find out how many of your men are ready to lay down their lives right now? Go ahead. Take a vote."

He did not want to take a vote. He was not that familiar with courage or heroics. He knew that each of the men in the room had acted heroically and courageously on many an occasion. But bravery in action was a thing dictated by the demands of the moment. Faced with certain death, would these men be willing to take an impossible gamble? He was not sure. But he felt fairly certain that given the choice "Your life or Carella's?" they would most probably choose to let Carella die. Selfish? Perhaps. Inhuman? Perhaps. But life was not something you could walk into a dime store to buy again if you happened to use one up or wear it out. Life was a thing you clung to and cherished. And even knowing Carella as he did, even (and the word was hard coming for a man like Byrnes) loving Carella, he dared not ask himself the question "Your life or Carella's?" He was too afraid of the answer he might give.

"How old are you, Virginia?"

"What difference does it make?"

"I'd like to know."

"Thirty-two."

Byrnes nodded.

"I look older, don't I?"

"A little."

"A lot. You can thank Carella for that, too. Have you ever seen Castleview Prison, Lieutenant? Have you ever seen the place Carella sent my Frank to? It's for animals, not men. And I had to live alone, waiting, knowing what Frank was going through. How long do you think youth lasts? How long do you think good looks hang around when you've got sorrow and worry inside you like a . . . like a *thing* that's eating your guts?"

"Castleview isn't the best prison in the world, but . . ."

"It's a torture chamber!" Virginia shouted. "Have you ever been inside it? It's dirty, filthy. And hot, and cramped, and rusting. It smells, Lieutenant. You can smell it for blocks before you approach it. And they crowd men into that hot filthy stench. Did my Frank cause trouble? Yes, of course he did. Frank was a man, not an animal — and he refused to be treated like an animal, and so they labeled him a troublemaker."

"Well, you can't . . ."

"Do you know you're not allowed to talk to anyone during work hours at Castleview? Do you know they still have buckets in each cell — *buckets* — no toilet facilities! Do you know what the stink is like in those sufferingly hot cubicles? And my Frank was sick! Did Carella think about that, when he became a hero by arresting him?"

"He wasn't thinking of becoming a hero. He was doing his job. Can't you understand that, Virginia? Carella is a cop. *He was only doing his job.*"

34

"And I'm doing mine," Virginia said flatly.

"How? Do you know what you're carrying in your goddamn purse? Do you realize that it might go up in your face when you fire that gun? Nitroglycerin isn't toothpaste!"

"I don't care."

"Thirty-two years old, and you're ready to kill a man and maybe take your own life in the bargain."

"I don't care."

"Talk sense, Virginia!"

"I don't have to talk sense with you or anyone. I don't have to talk at all." Virginia moved violently, and the purse jiggled in her lap. "I'm doing you a goddamn *favor* by talking to you."

"All right, relax," Byrnes said, nervously eyeing the purse. "Just relax, willya? Why don't you put that purse on the desk, huh?"

"What for?"

"You're bouncing around like a rubber ball. If you don't care about it going off, I do."

Virginia smiled. Gingerly, she lifted the purse from her lap, and gingerly she placed it on the desk top before her, swinging the .38 around at the same time, as if .38 and nitroglycerin were newlyweds who couldn't bear to be parted for a moment.

"That's better," Byrnes said, and he sighed in relief. "Relax. Don't get upset." He paused. "Why don't we have a smoke?"

"I don't want one," Virginia said.

Byrnes took a package of cigarettes from his pocket. Casually, he moved to her side of the desk, conscious of the .38 against the fabric of the purse. He gauged the distance between himself and Virginia, gauged how close he would be to her when he lighted her cigarette, with which hand he should slug her so that she would not go flying over against the purse. Would her instant reaction to the dropped match be a tightening of her trigger finger? He did not think so. She would pull back. And then he would hit her.

He shook a cigarette loose. "Here," he said. "Have one."

"No."

"Don't you smoke?"

"I smoke. I don't feel like one now."

"Come on. Nothing like a cigarette for relaxation. Here."

He thrust the package toward her.

"Oh, all right," she said. She shifted the .38 to her left hand. The muzzle of the gun was an inch from the bag. With her right hand, she took the cigarette Byrnes offered. Standing at her right, he figured he would extend the match with his left hand, let it fall into her lap, and then clip her with a roundhouse right when she pulled back in fright. Oddly, his heart was pounding furiously.

Suppose the gun went off when she pulled back?

He reached into his pocket for the matches. His hand was trembling. The cigarette dangled from Virginia's lips. Her left hand, holding the gun against the purse, was steady.

Byrnes struck the match.

And the telephone rang.

CHAPTER
FIVE

Virginia whipped the cigarette from her mouth and dropped it into the ash tray on her desk. She switched the gun back to her right hand and then whirled on Bert Kling who was moving to answer the telephone.

"Hold it, sonny!" she snapped. "What line is that?"

"Extension 31," Kling answered.

"Get away from this desk, Lieutenant," Virginia said. She gestured at him with the gun, and Byrnes backed away. Then, with her free hand, she pulled the telephone to her, studied its face for a moment, and then pushed a button in its base. "All right, answer it," she said, and she lifted her receiver the moment Kling did.

"Eighty-seventh Squad, Detective Kling."

He was very conscious of Virginia Dodge sitting at the next desk, the extension phone to her ear, the snout of the .38 pointed at the center of the big black purse.

"Detective Kling? This is Marcie Snyder."

"Who?"

"Marcie." The voice paused. "Snyder." Intimately, it whispered. "Marcie Snyder. Don't you remember me, Detective Kling?"

"Oh, yes. How are you, Miss Snyder?"

"I'm just fine, thanks. And how's the big blond cop?"

"I'm . . . uh . . . fine. Thanks."

He looked across at Virginia Dodge. Her lips were pressed into a bloodless smile. She seemed sexless, genderless, sitting opposite him with the lethal .38 pointed at the black hulk of the bag. And, in contrast to the thin shadow or death she presented, Marcie Snyder began to ooze life in bucketfuls. Marcie Snyder began to gyrate with her voice, undulate with her whispers so that Kling could visualize the big redhead lying on a chaise longue in a gossamer negligee, cuddling up to the ivory telephone in her hand.

"It's nice talking to you again," she said. "You were in such a hurry last time you were here."

"I had a date with my fiancée," Kling said flatly.

"Yes. I know. You told me. Repeatedly." She paused. Her voice dropped slightly. "You seemed nervous. What were you nervous about, Detective Kling?"

"Get rid of her," Virginia Dodge whispered.

"What?" Marcie said.

"I didn't say anything," Kling answered.

"I was sure I heard . . ."

"No, I didn't say anything. I'm rather busy, Miss Snyder. How can I help you?"

Marcie Snyder laughed the dirtiest laugh Bert Kling had ever heard in his life. For a moment, he felt as if he were sixteen years old and entering a whorehouse on La Via de Putas. He almost blushed.

"Come on," he said harshly. "What is it?"

"Nothing. We've recovered the jewels."

"Oh, yeah? How?"

"It turns out they weren't burglarized at all. My sister took them with her when she went to Las Vegas."

"Are you withdrawing the complaint then, Miss Snyder?"

"Why, yes. If there was no burglary, what have I got to complain about?"

"Nothing. I'm glad you located the jewels. If you'll drop us a letter to that effect, stating that your sister —"

"Why don't you come by and pick it up, Detective Kling?"

"I'd do that, Miss Snyder," Kling said, "but there's an awful lot of crime going on in this city, and I'm just about damn near indispensable. Thanks for calling. We'll be waiting for your letter."

He hung up abruptly, and then turned away from the phone.

"You're a regular lover boy, aren't you?" Virginia Dodge said, putting her receiver down.

"Yeah, sure. A regular lover boy," Kling answered.

He was, to be honest, embarrassed by the fact that Virginia had listened to Marcie Snyder's come-hither conversation. Bert Kling was twenty-five years old and not exactly adept at the sort of fencing Marcie Snyder did. He was a tall blond man with broad shoulders and a narrow waist, his face bearing the clean stamp of milk and strawberries. He was, in a sense, handsome — but his good looks were overshadowed by the innocence with which he carried them. Kling was engaged to a girl named Claire Townsend, whom he'd been dating steadily for the past year. He really wasn't interested in Marcie Snyder or her sister, or the countless Marcie

Snyders & Sisters to be found everywhere in the city. And so it annoyed him that Virginia Dodge might have thought he'd promoted this particular phone call. He didn't want her to think that.

He knew it was odd that he should care what a bitch like Virginia Dodge was thinking, but somehow it became a matter of pride to him that she should not think he was diddling around when he was supposed to be investigating a burglary.

He walked over to the desk where she sat. The black purse made him nervous. Suppose someone fell against it? Jesus, you had to be absolutely nuts to go around carrying a bottle of nitroglycerin.

"About that girl," he said.

"Yes?"

"Don't get the wrong idea."

"Why, what idea would that be?" Virginia Dodge said.

"Well, I mean . . . I was investigating a burglary, that's all."

"Why, what else *would* you be investigating, honey lamb?" Virginia asked.

"Nothing. Oh, forget it. I don't know why I'm bothering explaining it to you anyway."

"What's the matter with me?" Virginia said.

"Well, I wouldn't say you were exactly a stable person, would you? No offense meant, Mrs. Dodge, but the run-of-the-mill citizen doesn't run around waving a gun and a bottle of soup."

"Don't they?" Virginia was smiling now, enjoying herself immensely.

"Well, it's a slightly crazy stunt. I mean, even you have to admit that. I can see the gun, okay. You want to

40

kill Steve, that's your business. Listen, am I going to fight City Hall? But the nitro's a little dramatic, don't you think? How'd you manage to get it over here without blowing up half the city?"

"I managed," Virginia said. "I walked gently. I didn't sway my hips."

"Yeah, well, that's a good way to walk, I guess. Especially when you've got a high explosive in your bag, huh?" Kling smiled disarmingly. The clock on the wall read 5:33. It was beginning to get dark outside. Dusk spread across the sky, washing a deeper blue behind the color riot trees in the park. You could hear the kids shouting for a last inning of stickball before real darkness descended. You could hear mothers shouting from windows. You could hear men greeting each other as they entered bars for their before-dinner beers. You could hear all the sounds of life outside the grilled windows and you could hear, too — a sound as real as any of the others — the silence inside the squadroom.

"I like this time of day," Kling said.

"Do you?"

"Yes. Always did. Even when I was a kid. Something nice about it. Quiet." He paused. "Are you really going to shoot Steve?"

"Yes," Virginia said.

"I wouldn't," Kling said.

"Why not?"

"Well . . ."

"Is it all right to turn on some lights in here, Virginia?" Byrnes asked.

"Yes. Go ahead."

"Cotton, snap on the overheads. And can my men get back to work?"

"What kind of work?" Virginia asked.

"Answering complaints, typing up reports, making calls to . . ."

"Nobody makes any calls. And nobody picks up a phone unless I'm on the extension."

"All right. Can they type? Or will that disturb you?"

"They can type. At separate desks."

"All right, men," Byrnes said, "then let's do it. And listen to everything she tells you, and let's not have any heroics. I'm playing ball with you, Virginia, because I'm hoping you'll see reason before it's too late."

"Don't hold your breath," Virginia said.

"He's right, you know," Kling said softly, boyishly.

"Is he?"

"Sure. You're not doing yourself any good, Mrs Dodge."

"No?"

"No. Your husband's dead. You're not going to help him by killing a lot of innocent people. And yourself, too, if that soup should go off."

"I loved my husband," Virginia said tightly.

"Sure. I mean, Jesus, I should hope so. But what's the good of this? I mean, what are you accomplishing?"

"I'll be getting the man who killed him."

"Steve? Come on, Mrs. Dodge. You know he didn't kill your husband."

"I know nothing of the sort!"

"Okay, let's say he *did* kill him. I know that's not true, and you know it too — but we'll say it if it makes you happy, okay? So what do you accomplish by revenge?"

Kling shrugged boyishly. "Nothing. I'll tell you something, Mrs Dodge."

"Yes?"

"I've got a girlfriend. Her name is Claire. She's a dream. I'm gonna marry her soon. She's full of life, do you know? But she wasn't always that way. When I met her, she was dead. I mean dead, really *dead*. Do you know why?"

"Why?" Virginia asked.

"Why?"

"I'll tell you," Kling said boyishly. "She'd been in love with a fellow who got killed in Korea. And when he died, she let herself die, too. She went into this big shell, and she just wouldn't come out. A young girl! Hell, you can't be much older than she is. And in this shell." He shook his head. "She was wrong, Mrs. Dodge. She was so wrong. You see, she just didn't realize the guy was dead. She didn't realize the minute that bullet hit him, he wasn't the guy she loved any more, he was just another corpse. Dead! Finished! Out of it! She was carrying on an affair with a pile of fleshy rubble covered with maggots."

Kling paused and rubbed a hand over his chin.

"If you don't mind my saying so, you're doing the same thing."

"I'm not," Virginia said.

"Sure. Sure, you are. You're coming in here, and you're bringing the stink of death with you. Why, you know, you even *look* like Death, you know that? A pretty woman like you, and you've got death in your eyes and hanging around your lips. You're being stupid,

Mrs. Dodge. Really. If you were smart, you'd put up that gun and . . ."

"I don't want to hear any more," Virginia snapped.

"You think Frank would want you to do this? Get in all this trouble over him?"

"Yes! Frank wanted Carella dead. He said so. He hated Carella!"

"And you? Do you hate Carella, too? Do you even know him?"

"I don't care about him. I loved my husband. That's enough for me."

"But your husband was breaking the law when he got arrested. He *shot* a man! Now you couldn't expect Steve to give him a medal, could you? Now come on, Mrs. Dodge, be sensible."

"I loved my husband," Virginia said flatly,

"Mrs. Dodge, I'll tell you something else. You've got to make up your mind. Either you're a woman who really knows what love is all about, or else you're a cold-blooded bitch who's ready to blow this dump to hell and gone. You can't play both sides of the fence. Now which one is it?"

"I'm a woman. I'm here *because* I'm a woman."

"Then act like one. Put the gun up, and get the hell out of here before you get more trouble than you've had in all your life."

"No. No."

"Come on, Mrs. Dodge . . ."

Virginia stiffened in her chair. "All right, sonny," she said, "you can knock it off now."

"Wha . . . ?" Kling started.

"The big blue-eyed baby routine. You can just cut it. It didn't work."

"I wasn't trying to . . ."

"Enough," she said, "damnit, that's enough! Go find somebody else's tit to suck!"

"Mrs. Dodge, I . . ."

"Are you finished?"

The squadroom went silent. The clock on the squadroom wall, white-faced and leering, threw minutes onto the floor where they lay like the ghosts of dead policemen. It was dark outside the grilled windows now. The windows, half-way open to let in the October mildness, also let in the night sounds of early traffic. A typewriter started. Kling glanced toward the desk near one of the windows where Meyer had inserted a blue D.D. report together with two sheets of carbon and two duplicate report sheets into the machine. The hanging globe of light over Meyer cast a dull sheen onto his bald head as he hunched over the typewriter, pecking at the keys. Cotton Hawes walked to the filing cabinet and pulled open a drawer. The drawer squeaked on its rollers. He opened a folder and began leafing through it. Then he went to sit at the desk near the other window. The water cooler suddenly belched into the silence.

"I'm sorry I bothered you," Kling said to Virginia. "I should have known a person can't talk to a corpse."

There was a sudden commotion in the corridor outside. Virginia tensed where she sat at the desk. For an instant, Kling thought her finger would involuntarily tighten around the trigger of the .38.

"All right, inside, inside," a man's voice said, and Kling recognized it instantly as belonging to Hal Willis. He looked past the desk and into the corridor as Willis and his prisoner came into view.

The prisoner, to be more accurate, *burst* into view. Like the aurora borealis. She was a tall Puerto Rican girl with bleached blond hair. She wore a purple topcoat open over a red peasant blouse which swooped low over a threatening display of bosom. Her waist was narrow, the straight black skirt swelling out tightly over sinuously, padded hips. She wore high-heeled pumps, red, with black ankle traps. A gold tooth flashed in the corner of an otherwise dazzlingly white set of teeth. And, in contrast to her holiday garb, she wore no makeup on her face, which was a perfect oval set with rich brown eyes and a full mouth and a clean sweeping aristocratic nose. She was one of the prettiest, if flashiest, prisoners ever to be dragged into the squadroom.

And dragged she was. Holding one wristlet of a pair of handcuffs in his right hand, Willis pulled the girl to the slatted-rail divider while she struggled to retrieve her manacled wrist, cursing in Spanish every inch of the way.

"Come on, *cara mía*," Willis said. "Come on, *tsotzkuluh*. You'd think somebody was trying to hurt you, for Christ's sake. Come on, *Liebchen*. Right through this gate. Hi, Bert! something, huh! Hello, Pete, you like my prisoner? She just ripped open a guy's throat with a razor bl —"

Willis stopped talking.

There was a strange silence in the squadroom.

He looked first at the lieutenant, and then at Kling, and then his eyes flicked to the two rear desks where Hawes and Meyer were silently working. And then he saw Virginia. Dodge and the .38 in her hand pointed into the mouth of the black purse.

His first instinct was to drop the wristlet he was holding and draw his gun. The instinct was squelched when Virginia said, "Get in here. Don't reach for your gun!"

Willis and the girl came into the squadroom.

"*Bruta!*" the girl screamed. "*Pendega! Hijo de la gran puta!*"

"Oh, shut the hell up," Willis said wearily.

"*Pinga!*" she screamed. "Dirtee ro'n cop bastard!"

"Shut up, shut up, shut *up!*" Willis pleaded.

The girl was possibly three inches taller than Willis, who just cleared the minimum five-foot-eight height requirement for all policemen. He was, assuredly the smallest detective anyone had ever seen, with narrow bones and an alert cocker-spaniel look on his thin face. But Willis knew judo the way he knew the Penal Code, and he could lay a thief on his back faster than any six men using fists. He was, as he surveyed the gun in Virginia Dodge's hand, already figuring on how he could disarm her.

"What's up?" he asked the assembly at large.

"The lady with the gun has a bottle of nitro in her purse," Byrnes said. "She's ready to use it."

"Well, well," Willis said. "Never a dull moment, huh?" He paused and looked at Virginia. "Okay to take off my coat and hat, lady?"

"Put your gun on the desk here first."

"Thorough, huh?" Willis said. "Lady, you give me the chills. You really got a bottle of soup in that bag?"

"I've really got it."

"I'm from Missouri," Willis said, and he took a step closer to the desk.

For an instant, Kling thought the jig was up. He saw only Virginia Dodge's sudden thrust into the bag, and he tensed himself for the explosion he was certain would follow. And then her free hand emerged from the purse, and there was a bottle of colorless fluid in that hand. She put it down on the desk top gently, and Willis eyed it and said, "That could be tap water, lady."

"Would you like to find out whether it is or not?" Virginia said.

"Me? Now, lady, do I look like a hero?"

He walked closer to the desk. Virginia put her purse on the floor. The bottle, pint-sized, gleamed under the glow of the hanging light globes.

"Okay," Willis said, "first we check the gat." He pulled gun and holster off his belt and placed them very carefully on the desk top, his eyes never leaving the pint bottle of fluid. "This plays a little like Dodge City, doesn't it?" he said. "What's the soup for, lady? If I'd known you were having a blowout, I'd have dressed." He tried a laugh that died the moment he saw Virginia's face. "Excuse *me*," he said. "I didn't know the undertakers were holding a convention. What do I do with my prisoner, Pete?"

"Ask Virginia."

"Virginia, huh?" Willis burst out laughing. "Oh, brother, are we getting them today. You know what this one's name is? Angelica! Virginia and Angelica! The Virgin and the Angel!" He burst out laughing again. "Well, how about it, Virginia? What do I do with my angel here?"

"Bring her in. Tell her to sit down."

"Come on, Angelica," Willis said, "have a chair. Angelica! Oh, Jesus, that breaks me up. She just slit a guy from ear to ear. A regular little angel. Sit down, angel. That bottle on the desk there is nitroglycerin."

"What you mean?" Angelica asked.

"The bottle. Nitro."

"Nitro? You mean like a bom'?"

"You said it, doll," Willis answered.

"A bom'?" Angelica said. "*Madre de los cantos!*"

"Yeah," Willis said, and there was something close to awe in his voice.

CHAPTER
SIX

From where Meyer Meyer sat near the window typing his D.D. report, he could see Willis lead the Puerto Rican girl deeper into the squadroom to offer her one of the straight-backed chairs. He watched as Willis unlocked the handcuffs and then draped both wristlets over his belt. The skipper walked over and exchanged a few words with Willis and then, hands on hips, turned to face the girl. Apparently Virginia Dodge was going to allow them to question the prisoner. How kind of Virginia Dodge!

Patiently, Meyer Meyer turned back to his typing.

He was reasonably certain that Virginia Dodge would not walk over to his desk to examine his masterpiece of English composition. He was also reasonably certain that he could do what he had to do unobserved especially now that the Puerto Rican bombshell had exploded into the room. Virginia Dodge seemed completely absorbed with the girl's movements, with the girl's string of colorful epithets. He was sure, then, that he could carry out the first part of his plan without detection.

The thing he was not too sure of was his English composition.

He had never been a very good English student. Even in law school, his papers had never been what one would call brilliant. Somehow, miraculously, he had received his degree and passed his bar examinations only to receive a Greetings from Uncle Sam, advising him that he was to serve in the United States Army. After four years of trudging through muck and mire (Hello, Muck! Hello, Meyer!), he'd been honorably discharged. By that time, he'd decided that he didn't want to spend the next ten years of his life building a practice. Cubbyhole offices and ambulance chasing were not for Meyer Meyer. He had joined the police force and married the girl he'd been dating ever since his college days, Sarah Lipkin. (He could still remember the fraternity house banter: "Nobody's lips kin like Sarah's lips kin." The banter had never disturbed him. Patiently, he had smiled and listened to it. Patiently, he had continued dating her. Besides, the banter was true. Sarah Lipkin was the kissin'est fool he'd ever met. Maybe that was why he married her when he got out of the Army.)

His decision to leave the law profession startled Meyer. It startled him because he was usually a very patient man, and certainly it would have taken extreme patience to sit out the next ten years waiting for a client to step into the office. And yet, tossing patience aside for the first time in his life, he quit being a lawyer and joined the police force. In his own mind both professions were linked. As a cop, he would still be concerned with law. Patiently, doggedly, he did his job. He did not make Detective 3rd/Grade until he had been on the force for eight years. That took patience.

Patiently, he worked on his English composition now.

His patience was an acquired skill, nurtured over the years until it had reached a finely honed edge of perfection. He had certainly not been born patient. He had, however, been born with the attributes which would later make a life of patience an absolute necessity if he were to survive.

Meyer's father, you see, was a very comical man. That is to say, he considered himself something of a wit. Half of this consideration was perhaps erroneous. In any case, he was a tailor who played practical jokes on friends every now and then, to his vast enjoyment and their vast annoyance. When his wife, Martha, had already seemed past the age when she could have any further children, when — in fact — she was experiencing change of life, nature played its own practical joke on Meyer's father. Martha, of all things, was going to have another baby!

The news did not sit too well with Meyer's father. He thought dirty diapers and runny noses were all behind him and now, at this late stage of the game, another baby. He accepted the news with faintly disguised distaste, suffered through the pregnancy, and meanwhile plotted his own practical joke in retaliation against the vagaries of nature and birth control.

The Meyers were Orthodox Jews. At the *briss*, the classic circumcision ceremony, Meyer's father made his announcement. The announcement concerned the name of his new offspring. The boy was to be called Meyer Meyer. The old man thought this was exceedingly humorous. The *moile* didn't think it was so humorous. When he heard the announcement, his hand almost

52

slipped. In that moment, he almost deprived Meyer of something more than a normal name. Fortunately, Meyer Meyer emerged unscathed.

But being an Orthodox Jew in a predominantly Gentile neighborhood can be trying even if your name isn't Meyer Meyer. The repetitive-handle provided the hate-mongers with a ready-made chant: "Meyer Meyer, Jew on fire!" If the haters needed any further provocation for beating up the nearest Jew, Meyer's double-barreled name provided it. He learned to be patient. Patient, in the beginning, with his enemies. Later, when he realized how maliciously innocent had been his father's little joke, patient with his father. Patient, still later, with the young doctor who had originally diagnosed his mother's malignant cancer as a sebaceous cyst — a faulty diagnosis which had probably cost her life. And finally, patient with the world at large.

Patience is, perhaps, a rewarding virtue.

Patience leads to tolerance. A patient man is an easy going man.

But anger must erupt somewhere. Somehow, the body must compensate for years and years of learning to sublimate.

Meyer Meyer, at the age of thirty-seven, was completely bald.

Now, patiently pecldng at his typewriter, he composed his message.

"What's your name?" Byrnes asked the girl.

"What?" she said.

"Your name! *Cuál es su nombre?*"

"Angelica Gomez."

"She speaks English," Willis said.

"I don' speak Een-glés," the girl said.

"She's full of crap. The only thing she does in Spanish is curse. Come on, Angelica. You play ball with us, and we'll play ball with you."

"I don' know what means thees play ball."

"Oh, we've got a lallapaluza this time," Willis said. "Look, you little slut, cut the Marine tiger bit, will you? We know you didn't just get off the boat." He turned to Byrnes. "She's been in the city for almost a year, Pete. Hooking mostly."

"I'm no hooker," the girl said.

"Yeah, she's no hooker," Willis said. "Excuse me. I forgot. She worked in the garment district for a month."

"I'm a seamstress, that's what I am. No hooker."

"Okay, you're not a hooker, okay? You lay for money, okay? That's different. That makes it all right, okay? Now, why'd you slit that guy's throat?"

"What guy you speaking abou'?"

"Was there more than one?" Byrnes asked.

"I don' sleet nobody's thro'."

"No? Then who did it?" Willis asked. "Santa Claus? What'd you do with the razor blade?" Again, he turned to Byrnes. "A patrolman broke it up, Pete. Couldn't find the blade, though, thinks she dumped it down the sewer. Is that what you did with it?"

"I don' have no erazor blay." Angelica paused. "I don' cut nobody."

"You've still got blood all over your hands, you little bitch! Who the hell are you trying to snow?"

"That's from d'hanncuffs," Angelica said.

"Oh, Jesus, this one is the absolute end," Willis said.

The trouble, Meyer Meyer thought, is that it's hard to get the right words. It mustn't sound too melodramatic or it'll be dismissed as either a joke or the work of a crank. It has to sound sincere, and yet it has to sound desperate. If it doesn't sound desperate nobody'll believe it, and we're right back where we started. But if it sounds too desperate, nobody'll believe it anyway. So I've got to be careful.

He looked across the room to where Virginia Dodge was watching the interrogation of the Puerto Rican girl.

I've also got to hurry, he thought. She may just take it in her mind to amble over here and see what I'm doing.

"You know whose throat you slit?" Willis asked.

"I don' know nothin'."

"Then I'm gonna let you in on a little secret. You ever hear of a street gang called the Arabian Knights?"

"No."

"It's one of the biggest gangs in the precinct," Willis said. "Teen-age kids mostly. Except the guy who's leader of the gang is twenty-five years old. In fact, he's married and has got a baby daughter. They call him Kassim. You ever hear of anybody called Kassim?"

"No."

"In fiction, he's Ali Baba's brother. In real life, he's leader of this gang called the Arabian Knights. His real name is José Dorena. Does that ring a bell?"

"No."

"He's a very big man in the streets, Kassim is. He's really a punk — but not in the streets. There's a gang called the Latin Paraders and the shit has been on

55

between them and the Knights for years. And do you know what price the Paraders have set for a truce?"

"No. What?"

"An Arabian Knights jacket as a trophy — and Kassim *dead*."

"So who cares?"

"*You* ought to care, baby. The guy whose throat you slit is Kassim. José Dorena."

Angelica blinked.

"Yeah," Willis said.

"Is this legit?" Byrnes asked.

"You said it, Pete. So you see, Angelica, if Kassim dies, the Latin Paraders'll erect a statue of you in the park. But the Arabian Knights won't like you one damn bit. They're a bunch of mean bastards, sweetie, and they're not even gonna like the fact that you cut him — whether it leads to his untimely demise or not."

"What?" Angelica said.

"Whether he croaks or not, you're on their list, baby."

"I di'n know who he wass," Angelica said.

"Then you did do the cutting?"

"*Si*. But I di'n know who he wass."

"Then why'd you cut him?"

"He wass bodderin' me."

"How?"

"He wass try to feel me up," Angelica said.

"Oh, come on!" Willis moaned.

"He wass!"

"Dig the virgin, Pete," Willis said. "Why'd you cut him, baby? And let's not have the hearts and flowers this trip."

"He wass grab my bosom," Angelica said. "On the steps; In fron' the stoop. So I cut him."

Willis sighed.

Virginia Dodge seemed to be tiring of the inquisition. Nervously, she sat at the desk commanding a view of both squadroom and corridor beyond, the .38 in her hand, the clear bottle of nitroglycerin resting on the desk before her.

I have to hurry, Meyer thought. Get it all down once and for all with no mistakes, and then start moving. Because if she comes over here and sees this, she is just liable to pull the trigger and blow off the back of my head, and Sarah will be sitting *shivah* for a week. They'll have to cover every mirror in the house and turn all the pictures to the wall. God, it'll be ghastly. So get it done. October ain't a time for dying.

"He grabbed your bosom, huh?" Willis said. "Which one? The right one or the left one?"

"Iss not funny," Angelica said. "For a man he feels you up in public, iss not funny."

"So you slashed him?"

"*Sí.*"

"'Cause he grabbed for your tit, right?"

"*Sí*"

"What do you think, Pete?

"Dignity doesn't choose its professions," Byrnes said. "I believe her."

"I think she's lying in her teeth," Willis said. "We check around, we'll probably find out she's been making it with Kassim for the past year. She probably saw him looking at another girl, and so she put the blade to him. That's more like it, isn't it, baby?"

"No. I don' know thees Kassim. He jus' come over an' get fresh. My body iss my body. An' I give it where I want. An' not to peegs with dirty hans."

"Hooray," Willis said. "They're really gonna put a statue of you in the park." He turned to Byrnes. "What do we make it, Pete? Felonious assault?"

"What condition is this Kassim in?"

"They carted him off to the hospital. Who knows? He was bleeding all over the goddamn sidewalk. You know what killed me, Pete? A bunch of young kids were standing around in a circle. You could see they didn't know whether to cry or laugh or just scream. They were kind of hopping up and down, do you know what I mean? Jesus, imagine growing up with this every day of your life? Can you imagine it?"

"Keep in touch with the hospital, Hal," Byrnes said. "Let's hold the booking until later. We can't do much with . . ." He gestured with his head to where Virginia Dodge sat.

"Yeah. All right, Angelica. Keep your legs crossed. Maybe Kassim won't die. Maybe he's got a charmed life."

"I hope the son a bitch rots in his gray," Angelica said.

"Nice girl," Willis said, and he patted her shoulder. Meyer pulled the report from the typewriter. He separated the carbon from the three blue sheets, and then he read the top sheet. He read it carefully because he was a patient man, and he wanted it to be right the first time. There might not be another chance after this one.

The window near the desk was open. The meshed grill outside the window — which protected the glass from

58

the hurled brickbats of the 87th's inhabitants — would present only a small problem. Quickly, with one eye on Virginia Dodge, Meyer rolled the first report sheet into a long cylinder. Hastily, he thrust the cylinder through one of the diamond-shaped openings on the mesh and then shoved it out onto the air. He looked across the room.

Virginia Dodge was not watching him.

He rolled the second sheet and repeated the action.

He was showing the third and final sheet through the opening when he heard Virginia Dodge shout, "Stop or I'll shoot!"

DETECTIVE DIVISION REPORT

PLACE OF OCCURRENCE

THE DETECTIVES OF THE 87th SQUAD ARE

STREET

NAME OF PERSON REPORTING

BEING HELD PRISONER BY A WOMAN WITH
A GUN AND A BOTTLE OF NITROGLYCERIN.

GIVEN NAME   INITIALS

ADDRESS OF PERSON REPORTING

IF YOU FIND THIS NOTE, CALL HEADQUARTERS
AT ONCE! THE NUMBER IS CENTER 6-0800.

STREET

UNIFORM MEMBER ASSIGNED

HURRY!

DETECTIVE 2nd/GR MEYER

SURNAME   INITIALS   SHIELD NUMBER

ARRESTS

CHAPTER
SEVEN

Meyer whirled from the open window.

He fully expected a bullet to come crashing into him, and then he realized Virginia Dodge was not looking at him was not even facing in his direction. Hunched over, the .38 thrust out ahead of her, she had left the desk and the bottle of nitroglycerin and was standing a foot inside the slatted-rail divider.

On the other side of the divider was Alf Miscolo.

He stood undecided, his curly black hair matted to his forehead, his blue suspenders taut against his slumped shoulders, his shirt sleeves rolled up over muscular forearms. Total surprise was on his face. He had come out of the Clerical Office where he'd been sweating over his records all afternoon. He had walked to the railing and shouted, "Hey, anybody ready for chow?" and then had seen the woman leap from the desk with the gun in her hand.

He had turned to run, and she'd yelled, "Stop or I'll shoot!" and he'd stopped and turned to face her, but now he wondered whether or not he'd done the right thing. Miscolo was not a coward. He was a trained policeman who happened to be a desk jockey, but he'd learned to shoot at the academy and he wished now his gun was in his hand instead of in one of the filing cabinet drawers in the Clerical Office. The woman standing at the railing had the look of a crazy bitch on her face. Miscolo had seen that look before, and so he thought he'd been wise to stop when she yelled at him, and yet there were a lot of other men in that room and Jesus how long had she been here and was she going to shoot up the whole damn joint?

He stood in indecision for a moment longer.

He had a wife and a grown son who was in the Air Force. He did not want his wife to become a cop's widow, he did not want her making up beds in precincts, but, Jesus, that bitch had a crazy look on her face, suppose she shot everyone, suppose she went berserk?

He turned and started to run down the corridor.

Virginia Dodge took careful aim and fired.

She fired only once.

The bullet entered Miscolo's back just a little to the left of his spinal column. It spun him around in a complete circle and then slammed him up against the door to the Men's Room. He clung to the door for an instant and then slowly slid to the floor.

The bottle of nitroglycerin on the desk did not explode. There was, of course, no such thing as a locked-door murder mystery.

Steve Carella knew that with the instincts of an inveterate murder mystery reader and a true cop.

And yet here he was investigating a suicide which had taken place in a windowless room and — to make matters worse — the victim appeared to have hanged himself after locking the door from the inside. It had taken three strong men to snap that lock before they could enter the room. At least, that's what they had told him yesterday when he'd first investigated the case, and that's what they were telling him again today.

Maybe it is a suicide, Carella thought. The police department treats all suicides exactly like homicides, but that is only a formality. And maybe this is truly a suicide, what the hell, why should I always go around suspecting the worst of people?

The trouble is these sons of his all look as if they are capable of tripping a blind woman and cutting out her heart. And the old man left a fortune to be divided among them. And was it not possible that one of those sons — or maybe even all of them acting in concert — had decided to put the blocks to the old man and get that loot quick? According to the old man's lawyer, whom Carella had interrogated yesterday, the old man had left $750,000 in cash to be divided among "his beloved sons upon his death." That was a lot of scratch. Not to mention the whole of Scott Industries, Inc., and various other holdings throughout the country. Murders had certainly been committed for less.

But, of course, this was a suicide.

Why didn't he simply wrap it up as such? He was supposed to meet Teddy at the precinct at seven — hey, I'm going to have a baby, how about that? — and he certainly wouldn't get there in time if he hung around this creepy old mansion and tried to make a homicide out of an obvious suicide. Oh, was he going to wine and dine her tonight! Tonight, she'd be a queen, anything she wanted he would get for her.

Jesus, I love her, he thought.

So let's wrap the damn thing up and meet her on time, what say? What time is it anyway? He glanced at his watch. 5:45. Well, he still had a little time so he might just as well do a thorough job. Even if it didn't smell like suicide . . . oh, smell, smell, what the hell determines the smell of a case? Still, this one didn't smell like suicide.

The musty old mansion was an anomaly for the 87th Precinct. Built in the 1890s, it clung to the shoreline of the River Harb like a Charles Addams creation, hung with dark shutters, shrouded with a slate roof, its gables giving the house strange and shadowy angles. Not three miles from the Hamilton Bridge, it nonetheless gave the feeling of being three centuries removed from it. Time had somehow bypassed this eerie house squatting on the river's edge, its rusted iron fence erecting a barrier against society. The Scott Mansion. He could still remember taking the call yesterday.

"This is Roger . . . at the Scott Mansion. Mr. Scott has hanged himself."

Roger, of course, had been the butler, and so Carella immediately discounted him as a suspect. The butler never did it. Besides, he seemed more broken up over the old man's death than anyone else in the house. The old man, in any case, had not been a pretty sight to see. Obese in life, the coloration of death by strangulation had not enhanced his appearance at all.

They had led Carella to the storage room which the old man had converted into a private study, away from the larger study downstairs. The three sons — Alan, Mark, and David — had backed away from the door as

64

Carella approached it, as if the horror of that room and its contents was still terrifyingly fresh in their minds. The door jamb had been splintered. Pieces of splintered wood still rested on the floor outside the door. A crowbar was lying against the corridor wall.

The door opened outwards into the corridor. It opened easily when Carella tried it, but he saw instantly that the inside lock, a simple slip bolt, had been ripped from the door jamb when the door was forced. It hung from a single screw as he entered the room.

The old man lay in a crumpled fat ball at the opposite end of the room. The rope was still around his neck even though the sons had cut him down the moment they'd entered the room.

"We had to cut him down," Alan explained. "To get in. We used a crowbar to break the lock, but even then we had trouble getting the door open. You see, Father had tied one end of the rope to the doorknob before . . . before he hanged himself. Then he threw the rope over that beam in the ceiling and . . . well, after we forced the lock, we still had his weight to contend with, his weight pulling the door closed. We opened it a wedge with the crowbar, and then cut the rope before we could get in."

"Who cut the rope?" Carella asked.

"I did," Alan said.

"How'd you know the rope was there?"

"When we got the door open a crack, we could see the . . . the old man hanging. I stuck my arm into the opening and used a jackknife on the rope."

"I see," Carella had said.

Now, standing in the room where the hanging had taken place, he really tried to see. The old man, of course, had been carted away by the meat wagon yesterday — but everything else in the room was exactly as it had been then.

The room was windowless.

Nor were there any secret panels or passageways leading to it. He had made a thorough check yesterday. The walls, floor, and ceiling were as solid as Boulder Dam, constructed in a time when houses were built to last forever.

All right, the only way into this room is through that door, Carella told himself.

And the door was locked.

From the inside.

So it's suicide.

The old man had, indeed, fixed one end of the rope to the doorknob, thrown the length of rope over the ceiling beam, and then climbed onto a stool, fastened the rope to his neck, and jumped. His neck had not been broken. He had died of slow strangulation.

And surely his weight had helped to hold that door closed against the efforts of his three sons to open it. But his weight alone would not have resisted the combined pull of three brawny men. Carella had checked that with the laboratory yesterday. Sam Grossman, in charge of the lab, had worked it out mathematically, fulcrum and lever, weights and balances. Had the door not been locked, the brothers could have successfully pulled it open even with the old man's weight hanging at the end of the rope attached to the doorknob.

No, the door had to be locked.

There was physical evidence that it had been locked, too. For, had the slip bolt not been fastened against the retaining loop of metal, the lock would not have been ripped from the doorframe when the crowbar was used on it.

"We had to use the crowbar," Alan had said. "We tried to pull it open by force, and then Mark realized the door was locked from the inside, and he went out to the garage to get the crowbar. We wedged it into the door and snapped the lock."

"Then what?"

"Then Mark stepped up to the door and tried to open it again. He couldn't understand why it wouldn't open. We'd snapped the lock, hadn't we? We used the crowbar a second time, wedging the door open. That was . . . was when we saw Father. You know the rest."

So the door had been locked.

So it's suicide.

Or maybe it isn't.

What do we do now? Send a wire off to John Dickson Carr?

Wearily, Carella trudged downstairs, walking past the clutter of wood splinters still in the hallway outside the door.

He found Christine Scott in the small sitting room overlooking the River Harb. I don't believe any of these people's names, Carella thought. They've all popped out of some damn British comedy of manners, and they're all make-believe, and that old man up there *did* commit suicide and why the devil am I wasting my time questioning people and snooping around a musty garret room without any windows?

"Detective Carella?" Christine said.

She looked colorless against the flaming reds and oranges of the trees which lined the river bank. Her hair was an ash blond, almost silvery, but it gave an impression of lack of pigmentation. Her eyes, too, were a lavender-blue but so pastel as to be almost without real color. She wore no lipstick. Her frock was white. A simple jade necklace hung at her throat.

"Mrs. Scott," he said, "how are you feeling now?"

"Much better, thank you." She looked out at the flaming trees. "This is my favorite spot, right here. This is where I first met the old man. When David first brought me to this house." She paused. The lavender-blue eyes turned toward Carella. "Why do you suppose he killed himself, Detective Carella?"

"I don't know, Mrs. Scott," Carella said. "Where's your husband?"

"David? In his room. He's taking this rather hard."

"And his brothers?"

"Around the house somewhere. This is a very big house, you know. The old man built it for his bride. It cost seventy-five thousand dollars to build, and that was back in 1896 when money was worth a great deal more than it is now. Have you seen the bridal suite upstairs?"

"No."

"It's magnificent. Huge oak panels, and marble counter tops, and gold bathroom fixtures. And these wonderful windows that open onto a balcony overlooking the river. There aren't many houses like this one left in the city."

"Mmm, I guess not," Carella said.

Christine Scott crossed her legs, and Carella noticed them and thought, *She has good legs. The stamp of America. Legs without rickets. Firm fleshy calves and slender ankles and shoes that cost her fifty-seven-fifty a pair. Did her husband kill the old man?*

"Can I offer you a drink, Detective Carella? Is that allowed?"

Carella smiled. "It's frowned upon."

"But permitted?"

"Occasionally."

"I'll ring for Roger."

"Don't bother, please, Mrs. Scott. I wanted to ask you some questions."

"Oh?" She seemed surprised. Her eyebrows moved up onto her forehead, and he noticed for the first time that her eyebrows were black, and he wondered whether or not the ash blond hair was a bleach job, and he realized it probably was, no damn woman alive owned the impossible combination of ash blond hair and black eyebrows. Phony, he thought. Mrs. Christine Scott, who just stepped out of a British comedy of manners. "What kind of questions?"

"About what happened here yesterday."

"Yes?"

"Tell me."

"I was out back walking," Christine said. "I like to walk along the river. And the weather's been so magnificent, so much color, and such warm air . . ."

"Yes? Then what?"

"I saw Mark rush out of the house, running for the garage. I could tell by the look on his face that something was wrong. I ran over to the garage just as Mark came out with the crowbar. 'What's the matter?' I said."

"And what did he answer?"

"He said, 'Father's locked himself in the den and he won't answer us. We're going to force the door.' That was all."

"Then what?"

"Then he rushed back to the house, and I followed after him. David and Alan were upstairs, outside the door to Father's den. He was in there, you see, even though he's got a very large and beautiful study downstairs."

"Did he use the den often?"

"Yes. As a retreat, I suppose. He has his favorite books in there, and his music. A retreat."

"Was he in the habit of locking the door?"

"Yes."

"He always locked the door when he went up there?"

"As far as I know, yes. I know I've often gone up to call him for dinner or something, and the door's been locked."

"What happened when you came upstairs with Mark?"

"Well, Alan said they'd been trying to open the door, and it was probably locked, and they were going to force it."

"Did he seem anxious about your father-in-law?"

"Yes, of course he did. They'd been pounding on the door and making all sorts of noise and they'd got no answer. Wouldn't you have been anxious?"

"What? Oh, yes. Sure, I would. Then what?"

"They stuck the crowbar into the crack between door and jamb, and forced the lock."

"Then what?"

"Then Mark tried to open it, but it still wouldn't open. So they tugged on it and saw . . . saw . . ."

". . . that the old man had hanged himself, is that right?"

"Yes." Christine's voice dropped to a whisper. "Yes, That's right."

"Who was the first to notice this?"

"I was. I was standing a little bit away from them as they pried the door open. I could see the crack, and I saw . . . this . . . this figure hanging there, and I . . . I realized it was Father and I . . . I screamed!"

"Who noticed it next?"

"Alan did. And he took a knife out of his pocket and then reached into the room and cut the rope."

"And then the door opened easily, did it?"

"Yes."

"Then what?"

"They called Roger and asked him to phone the police."

"Did anyone touch anything in the room?"

"No. Not even Father."

"None of them went to your father-in-law?"

"They went to him, but they didn't touch him. They could see immediately that he was dead. David didn't think they should touch him."

"Why not?"

"Why, because he was dead."

"So?"

"He . . . he knew there would be policemen here, I suppose."

"But he also knew his father had committed suicide, didn't he?"

"Well . . . well, yes, I suppose so."

"Then why did he warn the others not to touch the body?"

"I'm sure I don't know," Christine said curtly.

Carella cleared his throat. "Do you have any idea how much your father-in-law was worth, Mrs. Scott?"

"Worth? What do you mean worth?"

"In property," Carella said. "In money."

"No. I have no idea."

"You must have some idea, Mrs. Scott. Surely you know he was a very wealthy man."

"Yes, of course I know that."

"But not *how* wealthy, is that right?"

"That's right."

"Did you know that he left $750,000 to be divided equally among his three sons. Not to mention Scott Industries, Inc., and various other holdings. Did you know that?"

"No. I didn't —" Christine stopped. "What are you implying, Detective Carella?"

"Implying? Nothing. I'm stating a fact of inheritance, that's all. Do you find the fact has implications?"

"No."

"Are you sure?"

"Yes, damnit, it has implications. It implies that perhaps someone deliberately . . . that's your damn implication, isn't it?"

"You're making the implications, Mrs. Scott. Not me."

"Go to hell, Mr. Carella," Christine Scott said.

"Mmm," Carella answered.

"You're forgetting one little thing, aren't you?"

"What's that?"

"My father-in-law was found dead in a windowless room, and the door was bolted from the inside. Now perhaps you can tell me how your implication of murder . . ."

"*Your* implication, Mrs. Scott."

". . . of murder ties in with what are obvious facts. Or do all detectives automatically go around looking for dirt? Is that your job, Mr. Carella? Looking for dirt?"

"My job is law enforcement. And crime detection."

"No crime has been committed here. And no law has been broken."

"Suicide is a crime against the state," Carella said flatly.

"Then you *do* admit it was suicide."

"It looks as if it might have been. But a lot of suicides that look like suicides turn out to be homicides. You don't mind if I'm thorough about it, do you?"

"I don't mind anything except your excess of bad manners. Provided you don't forget what I mentioned earlier."

"What's that?"

"That he was found in a windowless locked room. Don't forget that, Mr. Carella."

"Mrs. Scott," Carella said fervently, "I wish I *could*."

CHAPTER
EIGHT

Alf Miscolo lay crumpled against the door to the Men's Room.

Not thirty seconds had passed since the slug took him in the back. The people in the squadroom had frozen completely as if the explosion of the .38 had rendered them impotent, incapable of either speech or movement. The stench of cordite hung on the air with the blue-gray aftersmoke of the explosion. Virginia Dodge, in clear silhouette against the gray of the smoke, seemed suddenly to be a very real and definite threat. She whirled from the railing just as Cotton Hawes broke from his desk in the corner.

"Get back!" she said.

"There's a hurt man out there," Hawes said, and he pushed through the gate.

"Come back here or you're next!" Virginia shouted.

"The hell with you!" Hawes said, and he ran to where Miscolo lay against the closed door.

The bullet had ripped through Miscolo's back with the clean precision of a needle passing through a piece of linen. Then, erupting at its point of exit, it had torn a hole the size of a baseball just below his collarbone. The front of his shirt was drenched with blood. Miscolo was unconscious, gasping for breath.

"Get him in here," Virginia said.

"He shouldn't be moved," Hawes answered. "For God's sake, he . . ."

"All right, hero," Virginia said tightly; "the nitro goes up!" She turned back toward the desk swinging the gun so that it was dangerously close to the bottle of clear liquid.

"Bring him in, Cotton!" Byrnes said.

"If we move him, Pete, he's liable to . . ."

"Goddamnit, that's an order! Do as I say!"

Hawes turned toward Byrnes, his eyes narrowed. "Yes, *sir*," he said and there was barely concealed vehemence in his voice. He reached down for a grip on the prostrate Miscolo. The man was heavy, heavier now with unconsciousness. He could feel Miscolo's bulk as he lifted him from the floor, his muscular arms straining against the man's weight. He braced himself and then shoved Miscolo higher into his arms with a supporting knee. He could feel Miscolo's hot blood rushing against his naked forearm. Staggering with his load, he carried Miscolo through the gate and into the squadroom.

"Put him back there," Virginia said. "On the floor. Out of sight." She turned to Byrnes. "If anybody comes up here, it was an accident, do you hear me? A gun went off accidentally. Nobody was hurt."

"We're going to have to get a doctor for him," Hawes said.

"We're going to have to get *nothing* for him," Virginia snapped.

"The man's been . . ."

"Put him down, redhead! Behind the filing cabinets. And fast."

Hawes carried Miscolo to a point beyond the filing cabinets where the area of squadroom was hidden from the corridor outside. Gently, he lowered Miscolo to the floor. He was rising when he heard footsteps in the hallway beyond. Virginia sat at the desk quietly, putting her purse up in front of the bottle of nitro as a shield, and then quickly moving the pistol directly behind the bottle so that it too was hidden by the bag.

"Remember, Lieutenant," she whispered, and Dave Murchison, the desk sergeant came puffing down the hallway. Dave was in his fifties, a stout man who didn't like to climb steps and who visited the Detective Division upstairs only when it was absolutely necessary. He stopped just outside the railing, and then waited before speaking while he caught his breath.

"Hey, Lieutenant," he said, "what the hell was that? Sounded like a shot up here."

"Yes," Byrnes said hesitantly. "It was. A shot "

"Anything the . . . ?"

"Just a gun went off. By accident," Byrnes said. "Nothing to worry about. Nobody . . . nobody hurt."

"Jesus, it scared the living bejabbers out of me," Murchison said. "You sure everything's okay?"

"Yes. Yes, everything's okay."

Murchison looked at his superior curiously, and then his eyes wandered into the squadroom, pausing on Virginia Dodge, and then passing to where Angelica Gomez sat with her shapely legs crossed.

"Sure got a full house, huh, Loot?" he said.

"Yes. Yes, we're sort of crowded, Dave."

Murchison continued to look at Byrnes curiously. "Well," he said, shrugging, "long as everything's okay. I'll be seeing you, Pete."

He was turning to go when Byrnes said, "Forthwith."

"Huh?" Murchison said.

Byrnes was smiling thinly. He did not repeat the word.

"Well, I'll be seeing you," Murchison said, puzzled, and he walked off down the corridor. The squadroom was silent. They could hear Murchison's heavy tread on the metal steps leading to the floor below.

"Have we got any Sulfapaks?" Hawes asked from where he was crouched over Miscolo.

"The junk desk," Willis answered. "There should be one in there."

He moved quickly to the desk in the corner of the room, a desk which served as a catch-all for the men of the squad, a desk piled high with Wanted circulars, and notices from Headquarters, and pamphlets put out by the department, and two empty holsters, and a spilled box of paper clips, and an empty Thermos bottle, a fingerprint roller, an unfinished game of Dots, the scattered tiles of a Scrabble setup and numerous other such unfilable materials. Willis opened one of the drawers, found a first-aid kit and hurried to Hawes, who had ripped open Miscolo's shirt.

"God," Willis said, "he's bleeding like a stuck pig."

"That bitch," Hawes said, and he hoped Virginia Dodge heard him. As gently as he knew how, he applied the Sulfapak to Miscolo's wound. "Can you get something for his head?" he asked.

"Here, take my jacket," Willis answered. He removed it, rolled it into a makeshift pillow, and then — almost tenderly — put it beneath Miscolo's head.

Byrnes walked over to the men. "What do you think?"

"It isn't good," Hawes said. "He needs a doctor."

"How can I get a doctor?"

"Talk to her."

"What good will that do?"

"For Christ's sake, you're in command here!"

"Am I?"

"Aren't you?"

"Virginia Dodge has pounded a wedge into my command, Cotton, and split it wide open. As long as she sits there with her wedge — that damn bottle of soup — I can't do a thing. Do you want me to kill everyone in this room? Is that what you want?"

"I want you to get a doctor for a man who's been shot," Hawes answered.

"No doctor!" Virginia called across the room. "Forget it. *No doctor!*"

"Does that answer you?" Byrnes wanted to know.

"It answers me," Hawes said.

"Don't be a hero, Cotton. There're more lives in this than your own."

"I'm not particularly dense, Pete," Hawes said. "But what guarantee do we have that she won't fling that bottle when Steve arrives anyway? And even if she doesn't, what gives us the goddam right to sacrifice Steve Carella on our own petty selfish altars?"

"Would it be better to sacrifice every man in this room on Steve's altar?"

78

"Stop that talking over there," Virginia said. "Get on the other side of the room, Lieutenant! You, Shorty, over here! And you get in the corner, Redhead."

The men split up. Angelica Gomez watched them with an amused smile on her race. She rose then, her skirt sliding back over a ripe thigh as she did. Swiveling hip against hip socket, she walked over to where Virginia Dodge sat chastely with her gun and her bottle of nitroglycerin. Hawes watched them. He watched partially because he was mad as hell at the Skipper and he wanted to figure out a way of putting Virginia Dodge out of commission. But he watched, too, because the Puerto Rican girl was the most delicious-looking female he had seen in a dog's age.

In his own mind, he didn't know whether Angelica's buttocks interested him more than did the bottle of nitro on the desk. As he toyed with various plans for the bottle of nitro, he also toyed with various fantasies concerning the blonde's explosiveness, and as he fantasized he found that Angelica Gomez was more and more delightful to watch. The girl moved with contradictory economy and fluidity, slender ankle cowing into shapely calf and knee, hip grinding, flat simplicity of belly, firm rounded thrust of breast, sweeping curve of throat and jaw, aristocratic tilt of nose. She seemed absolutely at home within the specified confines of her body. It was a distinct pleasure to watch her. She was perhaps the most unself-conscious female he had ever met. At the same time, he reminded himself, she had slit a man's throat. A nice girl.

"Hey, ees that really a bom'?" Angelica asked Virginia.

"Sit down and don't bother me," Virginia answered.

"Don't be so touchy. I only ask a question."

"It's a bottle of nitroglycerin, yes," Virginia said.

"You gon' essplode it?"

"If I have any trouble, yes."

"Why?"

"Oh, shut up. Stop asking stupid questions."

"You got a gun, too, hah?"

"I've got *two* guns," Virginia said. "One in my hand, and another in my coat pocket. And a desk drawer full of them right here." She indicated the drawer to which she had earlier added Willis' gun.

"You minn business, I guess, hah?"

"I mean business."

"Hey, listen. Why you don' let me go, hah?"

"What are you talking about?"

"Why you don't let me walk out of here? You run the place, no? You hear the cop before, don't you? He say you put a wedge here, no? Okay. I walk out. Okay?"

"You stay put, sweetie," Virginia said.

"*Por qué?* What for?"

"Because if you walk out of here, you talk. And if you talk to the wrong person, all my careful planning is shot to hell."

"Who I'm gon' talk to, hah? I'm gon' talk to nobody. I'm gon' get the hell out the city. Go back Puerto Rico maybe. Take a plane. Hell, I slit a man's throat, you hear? All thees snotnose kids, they be after me now. I wake up dead one morning, no? So come on, Carmen, let me go."

"You stay," Virginia said.

"Carmen, don' be . . ."

"You stay!"

"Suppose I walk out, hah? Suppose I jus' do that?"

"You get what the cop got."

"Argh, you jus' mean," Angelica said, and she walked back to her chair and crossed her legs. She saw Hawes' eyes on her, smiled at him, and then immediately pulled her skirt lower.

Hawes was not really studying her legs. Hawes had just had an idea. The idea was a two-parter, and the first part of the idea — if the plan was to be at all successful — had to be executed in the vicinity where the Puerto Rican girl was sitting. The idea had as its core the functioning of two mechanical appliances, one of which Hawes was reasonably certain would work immediately, the other of which he thought might take quite some time to work if it worked at all. The idea seemed stunning in concept to Hawes and, fascinated with it, he had stared captured into space and the focus of his stare had seemed to be Angelica's legs.

Now, taking advantage of the girl's presence near the first of the appliances, realizing that Virginia Dodge had to be diverted before he could execute the first part of his plan, he ambled over to where Angelica sat and took a package of cigarettes from his shirt pocket.

"Smoke?" he said.

Angelica took the proffered cigarette. "*Muchas gracias*," she said. She looked up into Hawes's face as he lighted the cigarette for her. "You like the legs, hah, cop?" she said.

"Yeah, they're good legs," Hawes agreed.

"They dam' good legs, you bet," Angelica said. "You don' see legs like thees too much. *Muy bueno*, my legs."

"*Muy*," Hawes agreed.

Flatly, emotionlessly, Angelica Gomez said, "How you like to see the res' of me?"

If the phone rings, Hawes thought, Virginia will pick it up. She's listening in on conversations now, and she sure as hell won't let one get by her, not with the possibility that it might be Steve calling. And if her attention is diverted by a phone call, that'd be all the time I'd need to do what I have to do, to get this thing rolling so that the big chance can be prepared for later on. Assuming she acts impulsively, the way people will when they're . . . well, we're assuming a lot. Still, it's a chance. So come on, telephone, ring!

"I ask you a question," Angelica said.

"What was the question?"

"How you like to see the res' of me?"

"It might be nice," Hawes said.

His eyes were glued to the telephone. It seemed to him that during the course of the day, the telephone usually rang with malicious insistence every thirty seconds. Someone was always calling in to report a mugging or a beating or a knifing or a robbery or a burglary or any one of a thousand offenses committed daily in the 87th. So why didn't it ring now? Who had declared the holiday on crime? We can't stand a holiday right now — not with Steve waiting to walk into a booby trap, not with Miscolo bleeding from a hole the size of my head, not

82

with that bitch sitting with her bottle of nitro and her neat little .38.

"It be dam' nice," Angelica said, "an' tha's no bull. You see my bosom?"

"I see it."

Come on, phone! He could hear Angelica's words' and they drummed in his ears, but his ears were straining for another sound, the shrill sound of the telephone, and the squadroom seemed to be an empty vacuum waiting only for that single sound.

"Iss my real bosom," she said. "No bra. I got no bra on. You believe it?"

"I believe it."

"I show you."

"You don't have to. I believe it."

"So how 'bout it?"

"How about what?"

"You talk to the others, you let me go. Then you come see me later, hah?"

Hawes shook his head. "No dice."

"Why not? Angelica some piece," Angelica said.

Hawes nodded. "Angelica some piece," he agreed.

"So?"

"Number one. You see that lady sitting over there?"

"*Sí.*"

"She's not letting anyone out of here, some piece or not. Understand?"

"*Sí.* I mean when she iss gone."

"If she is *ever* gone," Hawes said. "And then I couldn't let you go anyway because that man standing over there near the bulletin board is the lieutenant in charge of this squad. And if I let you go, he might fire me or send me to prison — or even shoot me."

Angelica nodded. "It be worth it," she said. "Believe me. Angelica some stuff, believe me."

"I believe you," Hawes said.

He did not want to leave the girl because he had to be in her vicinity when the telephone rang, if it rang, wouldn't the damn thing ever ring? At the same time, he sensed that their conversation had reached a dead end, had come as far as it could possibly go. Stalling for time, he asked a timeless question.

"How'd you get to be a hooker, Angelica?"

"I no' hooker," she said. "Really."

"Now, Angelica," he said chidingly.

"Well, sometimes," she said. "But only to buy pretty clothes. I dress pretty, no?"

"Yes. Oh, yes."

"Listen, you come see me, hah? We make it."

"Honey," he said, "where you're going, they don't make anything but license plates."

"What?" she said, and the telephone rang.

The sound startled Hawes. He almost turned automatically to reach for the wall, and then he remembered that he had to wait until Virginia picked up the phone. He saw Byrnes start across toward the instrument on the desk nearest him. He saw Byrnes waiting for Virginia's nod before he picked up the receiver.

The phone kept shrilling into the squadroom.

Virginia shifted the gun to her left hand. With her right hand, she picked up the receiver and nodded toward Byrnes. Byrnes lifted his phone.

"Eighty-seventh Squad, Lieutenant Byrnes."

"Well, well, how come they've got the big cheese answering telephones?" the voice said.

Hawes edged toward the wall, backing toward it. Virginia Dodge was still partially facing him, so that he could not raise his hand. Then, slowly, she swiveled in the chair so that her back was to him. Swiftly, Hawes lifted his hand.

"Who is this?" Byrnes asked into the mouthpiece.

"This is Sam Grossman at the lab. Who the hell did you think it was?"

The thermostat was secured tightly to the wall. Hawes grasped it in one hand, and with a quick snap of his wrist raised the setting to its outermost reading.

On one of the mildest days in October, the temperature in the squadroom was now set for ninety-eight degrees.

CHAPTER
NINE

Sam Grossman was a detective, and a lieutenant, and a very thorough man. A less thorough man in charge of a police laboratory might have allowed his call to wait until the morning. It was, after all, three minutes to six, and Grossman did have a family waiting home to begin dinner. But Sam Grossman believed in laboratory work, and he believed in crime detection, and he believed that one went hand in hand with the other. Sam would never miss the opportunity to prove to his colleagues who did the actual legwork that the laboratory was a vital part of detection, and that they should use the lab as often as possible.

"The M.E. gave us a look at the corpse, Pete," he said into the phone now.

"What corpse?"

"The old man. Jefferson Scott."

"Oh, yes." "Carella working on that one?" Grossman said.

"Yes."

Byrnes glanced across to Virginia Dodge. She had sat up straighter in her chair at mention of Carella's name, and now she was listening intently to the conversation.

"He's a good man," Grossman said. "Is he out there at the Scott house now?"

"I don't know where he is," Byrnes said. "He might be. Why?"

"Well, if he is, it might be a good idea to get in touch with him."

"Why, Sam?"

"The M.E. set the cause of death as strangulation. You familiar with the case, Pete?"

"I've read Carella's report."

"Yeah, well, the old guy was found hanging. No broken neck or anything like that. Strangulation. Looked like suicide. Remember that Hernandez case a while back — where it looked like the kid had hanged himself, but it was really an overdose of heroin? Remember that one?"

"Yes."

"Well, we haven't got exactly the same thing here. This guy died of strangulation, all right "

"Yes?"

"But he wasn't strangled by the rope. He didn't hang himself."

"What happened then?"

"We've discussed this thoroughly with the M.E., Pete and we're pretty sure we're right. The bruises on the victim's throat indicate that he was strangled *manually* before that rope was placed around his throat. There are rope bruises and burns, too, but the majority of the bruises were left by human hands. We tried to get prints from the skin, but it didn't work. We're not always successful in getting prints from the skin of . . ."

"Then you think Scott was murdered?"

"Yeah," Grossman said flatly. "We also did some tests on that rope he was hanged with. Same as that Hernandez kid. The direction of the fibers on the rope show that he didn't jump *down* from that stool, the way it looked. He was *hauled* up. It's a homicide, Pete. No question about it."

"Mmm. Well, thanks a lot, Sam."

"The thing is," Grossman said; "if you think Carella's over at that Scott house, I'd contact him right away."

"I don't know if he's there," Byrnes said

"Well, *if* he is. Because *if* he is, one of the people in that house is a murderer with pretty big hands. And I like Steve Carella."

David Scott sat with his hands clenched in his lap. His hands were square and flat and covered with light bronze fuzz that curled along their backs. The same blondish bronze hair decorated the top of David's crewcut head. Behind him, far out on the river, the tugboats pushed their mournful night sound onto the air.

It was 6:10 P.M.

Before him sat Detective Steve Carella.

"Ever argue with the old man?" Carella asked.

"Why?" David said.

"I'd like to know."

"Christine has already told me a little about you and your ideas, Mr. Carella."

"Has she?"

"Yes. My wife and I keep no secrets from each other. She told me your mind is working along certain channels which I, for one, find pretty damn objectionable."

"Well, I'm awfully sorry you find them objectionable, Mr. Scott. Do you find homicide objectionable, too?"

"That's exactly what I meant, Mr. Carella. And I'd like to tell you this. We're the Scott family. We're not some slum foreigners living in a crawly tenement on Culver Avenue. We're the Scotts. And I don't have to sit here and listen to idle accusations from you because the Scotts have lawyers to take care of tin-horn detectives. So if you don't mind, I'd like to call one of those lawyers right now and . . ."

"*Sit down*, Mr. Scott!" Carella barked.

"Wh—?"

"Sit down, and get off that goddamn high horse! Because if you feel like calling one of those Scott lawyers you mentioned, you can damn well do it from the crawly squadroom of the 87th Precinct, which is where I'll take you and your wife and your brothers and anybody else who was in this house when the old man allegedly hanged himself."

"You can't . . ."

"I can, and I will! Now sit down."

"I . . ."

"Sit down!"

David Scott sat.

"That's better. I'm not saying your father didn't hang himself, Mr. Scott. Maybe he did. Suicides don't always leave notes, so maybe your father is a legitimate suicide. But from what I've been able to gather from Roger —"

"Roger is a servant who —"

"Roger told me that your father was a very jolly man who was interested in life and living. He had not seemed depressed over the past few weeks, and in fact he's very rarely known him to be depressed. Your father was a wealthy man with a giant corporation going for him, and holdings in sixteen of the forty-eight states. He's been a widower for twelve years, so we can't assume his suicide was caused through remorse for his dead wife. In short, he seemed to be a happy man with everything in the world to live for. Now suppose you tell me why a man like that would want to take his own life."

"I'm sure I don't know. Father wasn't much in the habit of confiding in me."

"No? You never talked to him?"

"Yes, of course I talked to him. But never intimately. Father was a cold person. Very difficult to know."

"Did you like him?"

"I loved him! He's my father, for God's sake."

"Which might, in modern psychiatric terms, be a good reason for hating him."

"I've been seeing a lay analyst for three years, Mr. Carella. I'm well-acquainted with psychology. But I did not hate my father. And I certainly had nothing to do with his death."

"Getting back . . . Did you ever quarrel with him?"

"Yes. Of course. Fathers and sons always have little squabbles, don't they?"

"Ever been up in that den of his?"

"Yes."

"Were you up there yesterday afternoon?"

"No."

"Not at all?"

"No. Not until we discovered the door was locked."

many times when Father locked the door. Do you see what I'm driving at?"

"Yes. If the bolt needed so much force, it would have been impossible to simply slide it closed from the outside using a piece of thread. I see what you mean."

"So let's assume I hated my father, if you will — which I didn't. Let's assume I was hungry for my share of the estate — which I wasn't. Let's assumed we all wanted him dead — which we didn't. The locked door still remains. The locked door with a slip bolt that needed all of a man's strength to close. No outside thread locked that door, Mr. Carella. It was locked from the inside. And knowing this to be the case, even you must admit that the only possible conclusion to be drawn is that my father committed suicide."

Carella sighed heavily.

The stores had closed at six, and Teddy Carella walked the streets now, debating whether or not she should stop for a cup of coffee. If she did, she might ruin her appetite. Steve had conjured visions of a sumptuous feast, and she was supposed to meet him at the squad at seven, and she certainly didn't want to spoil his plans simply because she desired a cup of coffee.

Besides, it was such a beautifully mild day, so marvelous for October.

October, she supposed, was her favorite month, even when the weather was behaving as seasonally as it should. It was the one month which really provided a feast for the eye, there I'm being prejudiced, I'm eliminating my worthless ears — that sounds Oriental —

in favor of my devouring eyes, well, I'm prejudiced, sue me.

I wonder how I'll look in maternity clothes.

Horrible.

Fat.

Will Steve love me?

Of course he'll love me, what a silly thing to wonder. Just because a woman swells up like a balloon and loses her waistline and develops sagging breasts and a big wide bottom and . . .

Oh my God, he'll *hate* me!

No. No, he'll love me. Love is enduring and love is good and love is would I love him if he suddenly weighed eight thousand pounds?

Yes, I would love him if he suddenly weighed ten thousand pounds. But he likes my figure and maybe . . . I won't take any chances. I'll stick to the diet, and I'll watch my weight, and I'll call on Lieutenant Byrnes and ask him to assign all the pretty-widow cases to the bachelors on the squad.

No cup of coffee, that settles that. The coffee in itself probably doesn't have too many calories, but the sugar certainly does. No coffee. I'll walk around and window shop, that's excellent for the figure.

Or maybe I should go up to the squad now?

Maybe Steve'll be back earlier than he thought. I could surprise him. Yes, maybe I'll do that. Go up to the squad now and wait for him. I'll think about it.

He might like a surprise waiting when he walks into the squadroom.

The man walked with his head bent.

There was no breeze blowing, not a strong breeze in any case, only a mild caressing murmur of air, but he walked with his head bent because he never really felt quite like himself in this city, never really felt quite like a person. And so he ducked his head, pulling it into his shoulders as far as he could, almost like a turtle defending himself against any blow which might come.

The man was nicely dressed. He wore a tweed suit and a neat blue tie fastened to his white shirt with a tiny gold pin. He wore dark blue socks, and black loafers, and he knew he looked like any other man walking the streets, and yet he did not feel as if he were a real person here, an individual, a person who could walk with his head up and his shoulders back — the city had done that to him, the city had given him this feeling of not belonging, not *being*. And so he walked with his hands in his pockets and his head bent.

And because his head was bent, he happened to notice the blue sheet of paper lying on the sidewalk. And because he was in no particular hurry to get anywhere in this city of hostility which made him feel unimportant, he picked up the paper and studied it with curious brown eyes.

The blue sheet of paper was the original Detective Division Report which Meyer Meyer had typed and floated down from the second-storey window of the precinct house. The two carbon copies of the D.D. form were nowhere in sight on the sidewalk. There was only the one blue sheet, and the man picked it up and studied it, and then walked to one of the big trash baskets sitting under the lamp-post on the corner of the block. The trash basket read KEEP OUR CITY CLEAN.

The man crumpled Meyer Meyer's message and hurled it into the trash basket. Then he put his hands into his pockets, ducked his head, and walked on his way in this hostile city.

The man's name was Juan Alverra, and he had arrived from Puerto Rico three months ago. No one in the city had attempted to teach Juan the English language which Meyer had used to compose his note.

Juan Alverra read and wrote only Spanish.

CHAPTER
TEN

Cotton Hawes unobtrusively closed first one window and then the other. Outside, the sultry night pressed its blackness against the windowpanes, filtered by the triangular mesh beyond the glass. The six hanging light globes, operated by a single switch inside the railing near the coat rack, feebly defended the room against the onslaught of darkness. A determined silence had settled over the squadroom, the silence of waiting.

Angelica Gomez sat with her crossed legs and high-heeled pumps, jiggling one foot impatiently. Her coat was draped over the back of her chair. Her peasant blouse swooped low over her confessedly unrestricted bosom. She sat with her own thoughts — thoughts perhaps of the man whose throat she'd cut, a man named Kassim whose friends had behind them the power of the vendetta; thoughts perhaps of the uncompromising arm of the law; thoughts perhaps of an uncomplicated island in the Caribbean where the sun had always shone and where she had helped cut sugar cane in season and drunk deeply of rum at night with the guitars going in the velvet black hills.

At the desk beside her sat Virginia Dodge, solemnly dressed in black — black dress and black overcoat and black shoes and black leather tote bag. Thin white legs and a thin white face. The blue-black steel of a revolver in her fist. The colorless oil of a high explosive on the desk before her. Nervously, the fingers of her left hand rapped a tattoo on the desk top. Her eyes, so brown that they too appeared black, darted about the room, wild birds searching for a roost, settling always on the corridor beyond the railing, waiting for the appearance of a detective who had sent her man to prison.

Behind her, on the floor near the huge green bulk of the metal filing cabinets, lay Alf Miscolo, police clerk. Unconscious, gasping for breath, his chest and head on fire, Miscolo did not know he might be dying. Miscolo knew nothing. In the void of his unconsciousness, he dreamt he was a boy again. He dreamt that it was Hallowe'en, dreamt that he was carrying bundles of paper to be tossed into the huge bonfire set in the middle of the city street. He dreamt he was happy.

Cotton Hawes wondered if the room were getting any hotter.

It was difficult to tell. He was sweating profusely, but he was a big man, and he always did sweat when the pressure mounted. He had not sweated much when he was a detective assigned to the 30th Squad. The 30th was a posh precinct and he had not, in all truth, relished his transfer to the 87th. The transfer had come through in June, and now it was October — four paltry months — and here he was a part of the 87th, working with the men

98

here, knowing the men here, deeply concerned about the welfare of a single solitary man named Steve Carella.

Perhaps the lieutenant was right. Misunderstanding Byrnes' thinking, Hawes assumed he was willing to let Carella die for the safety of the other men on the squad, and perhaps Byrnes' reasoning was right. Perhaps it was perfectly moral and perfectly logical to allow Carella to walk into the blazing end of a .38. But Hawes did not believe so.

The 87th, he'd discovered, was a strange precinct and a strange squad. He had approached the transfer with great hostility, rejecting the concept of slums and slum dwellers, rejecting the men of the squad, chalking them off as disillusioned cynics even before he'd met them. He had learned otherwise, and very quickly.

He had learned that the people of the slums were only people. They enjoyed the same pleasures he did, and they suffered a great many misfortunes he would never have to suffer. They wanted love, and they wanted respect, and the walls of a tenement did not necessarily become the cage of an animal. He had learned this from the men of the squad. He had seen each and every one of them in action. He knew that they held no rose-colored-glasses view of the precinct or its crime rate. He knew they could knock a thief flat on his back without batting an eyelid and without any great amount of soul-searching afterwards. Crime was crime, and no cop of the 87th tried to rationalize the evil of crime.

But he was surprised to learn that the men of the 87th clung to another concept which in no way limited the effectiveness of their law enforcement; that concept was fairness. And within this concept, they knew when to get tough and when to understand. They did not automatically equate slum dwellers with criminals. A thief was a thief — but a person was a person. Fairness. And he had found the concept a contradictory one for men confronted daily with the facts of violence and sudden death.

And now, in the squadroom where fairness was an unspoken credo, the men had been presented with a situation which was totally unfair, totally illogical, and yet it sat there. Immovable, illogical, unfair, it sat there and waited.

Perhaps there was a primitive justice to the reasoning of Virginia Dodge. An eye for an eye, a tooth for a tooth, had not the Bible so specified? Hawes' father had been a religious man, a man who'd felt that Cotton Mather was the greatest of the Puritan priests, a man who'd named his son in honor of the colonial God-seeker who'd hunted witches with the worst of them.

Jeremiah Hawes had chalked off the Salem witch trials as the personal petty revenges of a town feeding on its own ingrown fears. He had exonerated Cotton Mather and the role the priest had played in bringing the delusion to its fever pitch.

And now, Virginia Dodge was engaged in her own witch hunt. Revenge. Steve Carella had done her an irreparable ill by sending her husband to prison, where he'd died. Perhaps the good Reverend Parris in 1692 had felt, too, that the townspeople of Salem had done him the same ill when they'd haggled over the amount of firewood he'd need to get through the winter. Perhaps the Reverend Parris had all unconsciously fed the fires of the hunt in an attempt to strike back at the petty people of the town. There was no such element of unconscious behavior in the actions of Virginia Dodge. She had come here to do murder, she had come here to satisfy a consuming desire for revenge.

There had been sane people in 1692. There were sane people in this squadroom today. And yet the sane ones had allowed the "witches" to be hanged. And would the sane ones here, today, in the face of the judgment of Virginia Dodge, fanatic, allow Steve Carella to be hanged?

I wonder if it's getting any hotter? Hawes thought.

He looked across the room and saw that Willis had unloosened his tie. He hoped desperately that — if the room were truly getting hotter — none of the men would mention the heat, none of them would go to the thermostat and lower it to a normal setting.

Leaning against the bulletin boards near the coat rack, Lieutenant Byrnes watched Hawes with narrowed eyes.

Of all the people in the room, Byrnes had been the only one to see Hawes raise the thermostat. Talking with Grossman on the telephone, he had watched Hawes as he stepped swiftly to the wall and twisted the dial on the instrument. Later, he had seen Hawes when he closed both windows, and he knew then that Hawes had something on his mind, that both actions were linked and not the idle movements of a thoughtless man.

He wondered now what the plan was.

He also wondered who or what would screw it up.

He had seen the action, but he was reasonably certain no one else in the room had followed it. And if Hawes was banking on heat, who would soon comment on the heat? Anyone might. Bert Kling had already taken off his jacket and was now mopping his brow. Willis had pulled down his tie. Angelica Gomez had pulled her skirt up over her knees like a girl sitting on a park bench trying to get a breeze from the river. Who would be the first to say, "It's hot as hell in here?"

And why did Hawes want heat to begin with?

He knew that Hawes had misunderstood him. He felt somewhat like a man falsely accused of racial prejudice because of a misunderstood remark. Hawes, of course, had not been attached to the 87th at the time of the Hernandez kill. Hawes did not know that Carella had risked his life for Byrnes' son, had come very close to losing that life. Hawes did not know how strong the bond was between Byrnes and Carella, did not know that Byrnes would gladly face a cannon if he thought it would help Steve.

But Byrnes was faced with the problem of command. And using the timeless logic of generals in battle, he knew that he could not be concerned over the welfare of a single man when the lives of many other were at stake. If Virginia Dodge's single weapon were that .38, he'd have gladly sacrificed himself on its muzzle. But she also held a bottle of high explosive.

And if she fired at the bottle, the squadroom would go up and with it every man in the room He owed a lot to Carella, but he could not — as commanding officer of the squad — try a gamble which would endanger every life for a single life.

He hoped now that Hawes' plan was not a foolhardy one.

And, sourly, he thought, *Any* plan is a foolhardy one with that bottle of nitro staring at us.

Bert Kling was beginning to sweat.

He almost walked over to the windows and then he remembered something.

Hadn't Cotton just walked over there to *close* them?

Hadn't he just seen Cotton . . . ?

And wasn't the temperature in the room controlled by thermostat? Had someone raised the thermostat? Cotton?

Did Cotton have a plan?

Maybe, maybe not. In any case, Bert Kling would melt right down into a puddle on the wooden floor before he opened a window in the joint Curiously, he waited. Profusely, he sweated.

Hal Willis was about to comment on the rising temperature in the room when he noticed that Bert Kling's shirt was stained with sweat. Their eyes locked for a moment. Kling wiped a hand across his brow and shook perspiration to the floor.

In an instant of mute understanding, Hal Willis realized that it was *supposed* to be getting hotter in the room.

He searched Kling's eyes, but there was no further clue in them.

Patiently, his underwear shorts beginning to stick to him, he wiggled on his chair and tried to make himself more comfortable.

Meyer Meyer wiped the beaded sweat from his upper lip.

It's hot as hell in here, he thought. *I wonder if anybody found my notes.*

Why doesn't somebody turn down the goddam heat? he thought. He glanced over at the thermostat. Cotton Hawes was standing near the wall, his eyes fastened to Virginia Dodge. He looked for all the world like a sentry guarding something. What the hell was he guarding?

Hey, Cotton, he thought, *reach over and lower that damn thermostat, will you?*

The words almost reached his tongue.

And then he wondered again if anyone had found his notes.

And, wondering this, his mind drifted away from thoughts of the heat in the room and — oddly for a man who had not been inside a synagogue for twenty years — he began to pray silently in Hebrew.

Angelica Gomez spread her legs and closed her eyes.

It was very hot in the room, and with her eyes closed she imagined she was lying on a rock in the mountains with the sun beating down flatly on her browned body. In Puerto Rico, she would climb trails as old as time, trails hidden by lush tropical growth. And then she would find a hidden glade, a glade wild with ferns. And in that glade, there would be a level rock, and she would take off all her clothes and tilt her breasts to be kissed by the sun.

Idly, she wondered why there was no sun in the streets of the city.

Lazily, she kept her eyes closed and allowed the heat to surround her. Suspended, her mind in the Caribbean, she relished the heat and hoped no one would open a window.

The telephone rang.

Seated at her command desk, her brow hung with tiny globes of perspiration, Virginia Dodge nodded to Kling who picked up a receiver and waited for her to follow suit. She nodded again.

"Eighty-seventh Squad, Detective Kling."

"Hello. Carella there?"

"Who's this?"

"Atchison at the lab. Where's Carella?"

"Out. Can I take a message?"

"Yeah, I suppose so. What'd you say your name was?"

"Bert Kling."

"I don't think I know you."

"What difference does it make?" Kling asked.

"I like to know who I'm dealing with. Listen, on this Scott kill?"

"Yeah?"

"Sam Grossman gave me some photos to study. Of the door jamb?"

"Yeah?"

"You familiar with the door jamb?"

"Carella's talked to me about it. Give me the information and I'll pass it on to him."

"What's your hurry? Don't you like conversation?"

"I dote on it. But we're a little busy here right now."

"I like conversation," Atchison said. "Breaks the monotony. You should have to sit here all day with test tubes and photographs and fluorescent light. You should have to examine clothes that stink of blood and pus and and piss all day long. Then you wouldn't mind a little conversation."

"I bleed for you," Kling said. "What about the door jamb?"

"I should be home right now. Instead, I've been blowing up pictures all day long, trying to help you mugs. That's the gratitude I get."

"I'll send you some of my old laundry so you can check for laundry marks. How's that?" Kling said.

"That's very funny. Be sure it's unwashed laundry, like the kind we always get. The kind that stinks of blood and pus and . . ."

"Yeah, I get the picture."

"What'd you say your name was?"

"Bert Kling."

"You're a comedian, huh, Kling?"

"Kling and Cohen, haven't you heard of us?"

"No," Atchison said flatly.

"Bird calls, dance routines, and snappy patter. We play *bar mitzvahs* and Irish weddings. You've never heard of Kling and Cohen?"

"Never. Is that supposed to be another joke?"

"I'm making conversation. That's what you're hungry for, isn't it?"

"Don't be so damn obliging. Someday you'll come in here and want a favor, and I'll throw a bag of laundry at you."

"What about the door jamb?"

"Maybe I shouldn't even tell you. Let you sweat it out on your own."

"Okay, suit yourself."

"Sure, and Sam would blow a gasket. What's with him and this Carella? You'd think he was his son-in-law or something, the way he's knocking himself out here."

"No," Kling said. "Steve's his father. There's a strong father-son relationship there."

There was a long pause on the line. Then, in a flat voice, Atchison said, "For the sake of the act, I hope Cohen is funnier than you. You want to take down this dope?"

"I've been waiting," Kling said.

"Okay. I blew up the photos and studied them. There are markings on the inside of the door jamb, where the lock was hanging loose. It was hanging by one screw, do you follow, allegedly snapped off when the guys there used a crowbar on the door."

"Go ahead."

"Well, it looks at though somebody used either a chisel or a screwdriver to pry that lock loose from the *inside*."

"What are you saying?"

"That the crowbar used on the outside didn't rip that lock loose. There's evidence that it was torn off from the inside. The jamb's all marked up. The guy who did it was probably in pretty much of a hurry."

"You're saying the door *wasn't* locked."

"That's what I'm saying."

"Then why couldn't they open it?"

"That's the sixty-four dollar question, Mr. Kling. Why couldn't three strong guys open a door that wasn't locked? We thought maybe the body hanging like that held it closed. But three strong men could have pulled it open in spite of the body. Either that, or the rope would have snapped. So it ain't that."

"Then what is it?"

"Tell you what you do," Atchison said.

"Yeah."

"Ask Cohen," and he hung up.

Kling replaced the receiver on the cradle. Virginia Dodge put down her phone.

"Is there any way of reaching Carella?" she asked.

"No. I don't know where he is," Byrnes lied.

"Shouldn't he have all this information that's pouring in?"

"Yes."

"Then why don't you call to give it to him?"

"Because I don't know where he is."

"Wouldn't he be at this Scott house? That's where the murder was committed, isn't it?"

"Yes, that's right. But if he's interrogating suspects, he could be anywhere."

"Why don't we try the Scot house?"

"What for?"

"Because if he's there, I want you to tell him to come back to the station house immediately. It's hot as hell in here, and I'm getting tired of waiting."

"I don't think he's there," Byrnes said quickly. "Besides, if I pull him back to the squad, he'll think something's fishy."

"Why should he think that?"

"Even you should realize that homicide gets priority over anything else."

Virginia Dodge thought this over for a moment. "I wish I knew whether or not you're lying," she said. But she did not ask Byrnes to make the call.

Sitting behind the high desk downstairs in the muster room, the desk which looked almost like a judge's altar of justice, the desk which had a sign requesting all visitors to stop there and state their business, Dave Murchison looked through the open doors of the station house to the street outside.

It was a beautiful night, and he wondered what ordinary citizens were doing on a night like this. Walking through the park with their lovers? Screwing with the windows open? Playing bingo or mah-jongg or footsie?

They certainly weren't sitting behind a desk answering telephones.

Now what the hell had the lieutenant meant?

Murchison tried to reconstruct the dialogue in his own mind. He had gone upstairs to see what the hell the noise had been about, and the loot had said it was just an accident, and he had said something about well, so long as everything's okay, and the loot had said yes, everything's fine or something like that and then . . . now here was the important part, so let's get it straight.

He had said to the loot, "Well, long as everything's okay. I'll be seeing you, Pete."

And Byrnes had answered, "Forthwith."

Now that was a very strange answer for the loot to give him because in police jargon "Forthwith" meant "Report immediately."

Now how could he report immediately if he was already standing there in front of the lieutenant?

So, naturally, he had said, "Huh?"

And the loot hadn't said anything in answer, he had just stood there with a kind of sick smile on his face.

Forthwith.

Report immediately

Had the loot meant something? Or was he just clowning around?

And if he meant something, what did he mean? Report immediately. Report to *whom* immediately? Or maybe report *something* immediately. Report *what*?

The gun going off?

But the loot said that was an accident, and everything sure as hell looked copacetic upstairs. Did he want him to report the accident? Was that it?

No, that didn't make sense. A gun going off by accident wouldn't make the loot look too good, and he certainly wouldn't want that reported.

Argh, I'm making too much of this, Murchison thought. The loot was having his little joke, and here I'm trying to figure out what he meant by a gag. I should be upstairs working with the bulls, that's what. I should have been a detective, trying to figure out the meaning of a stupid little thing the loot tells me. It must be this Indian summer. I should be back in Ireland kissing Irish lasses.

Forthwith.

Report immediately.

A light on Murchison's switchboard exploded into green. One of the patrolmen was calling in. He plugged in his socket and said, "Eighty-seventh Precinct, Sergeant Murchison. Oh, hello, Baldy. Yep. Okay, glad to hear it. Keep on your toes."

All quiet on the Western front, Murchison thought. He pulled the wire from the board.

Forthwith, he thought.

Virginia Dodge rose suddenly.

"Everybody over there," she said. "That side of the room. Hurry up Lieutenant, get away from that coat rack."

Angelica stirred, rose, smoothed her skirt over her hips, and walked toward the grilled windows. Hawes left his post by the thermostat to join the other men who began drifting toward the windows. Byrnes moved away from the coat rack.

"This gun stays trained on the nitro," Virginia said, "so no funny stuff."

Good! Hawes thought. *She's not only thinking of the heat, she's also worried about the nitro. It's going to work. Jesus, the first part of it is going to work.*

I hope.

Virginia backed toward the coat rack. Quickly, she skipped the coat off her left shoulder, the gun in her right hand aimed at the nitro on the desk. Then she shifted the gun to her left hand, slipped the coat off her right shoulder and, without turning, hung it on one of the pegs on the rack.

"It's hot as hell in here," she said. "Can't someone lower the heat?"

"I will," Hawes said, and he went immediately to the thermostat.

There was a grin on his face. He looked across the room to where Virginia Dodge's shapeless black coat hung alongside Willis' hat and coat on the rack.

In the lefthand pocket of Virginia's black garment was the pistol she had taken from Lieutenant Byrnes' office.

CHAPTER
ELEVEN

It was remarkable, Hawes thought, how simply it had worked. If everything in life worked as easily as the first part of his plan had, everyone in the world would have his own private pink cloud upon which to float around. But the very ease with which Virginia had taken off her coat and parted with the pistol gave him his first twinge of doubt. He was not a superstitious man, but he regarded simplicity of action with some skepticism. Was the success of the first part an ill omen for the second part?

Anxiously he began to review the plan in his mind.

The gun was now where he wanted it, in the pocket of a coat hanging on the rack near the bulletin board. Between the coat rack and the bulletin board, on the short stretch of wall inside the slatted railing, was the light switch which controlled the overhead globes. It was Hawes' idea to amble over to the bulletin board, busy himself with taking down some notes from the Wanted circulars and then — when and if the opportunity presented itself — snap out the lights and reach for Byrnes' pistol in the coat. He would not use the pistol immediately because he did not want a long-distance shooting duel, not with that bottle of nitro on the desk in front of Virginia. He would hold the pistol until it was safe to fire it without the attendant possibility of a greater explosion.

He did not see how the plan could fail. The switch controlled every light in the room. One flick, and the lights would go out. It would take him no more than three seconds to snatch the gun, hide it, and click on the lights again.

Would Virginia Dodge fire at the nitro in those three seconds?

He did not believe so.

In the first place, even if she did fire, the room would be in total darkness and she probably wouldn't be able to hit the bottle.

Well, that's a hell of a gamble to be taking, he told himself. She doesn't even have to fire at it, you know. All she has to do is sweep it off the desk with her arm, and there goes eternity.

But he was banking on something else, a person's normal reaction to a suddenly darkened room. Wouldn't Virginia, in the confusion of the moment, assume there'd been a power failure or something? Wouldn't she hold her fire, hold the sweeping motion of her arm at least long enough to be certain one way or the other? And by that time, the lights would be on again and Hawes could invent some excuse about having turned them off by accident.

It had better be a damn good excuse, he told himself.

Or did it really have to be a good one? If, when the lights went on again, everything was apparently as it had been before the darkness, wouldn't she accept any alibi?

Or would she remember the gun in the coat pocket? Wed, if she did, they'd have it out then and there, nitro or no nitro. And at least they'd be evenly matched, a pistol for a pistol.

Again, he went over the steps in his mind. Get to the bulletin board, busy myself there, click out the lights, grab the gun . . .

Now wait a minute.

There was an alternate switch at the far end of the corridor, just at the head of the metal steps. This switch, too, controlled the lights in the corridor and the squadroom so that it wasn't necessary to walk the entire length of the hall in complete darkness when coming onto the second floor of the building. But Hawes wondered if he had to do anything to that second switch in order to ensure "darkness in the squadroom when he made his play. He did not think so. Each switch, he hoped, worked independently of the other, both capable of either turning on or extinguishing all the lights. In any case, it had better work that way. Virginia Dodge had already used her gun once, and she showed no signs of reticence about pulling the trigger again.

Well, he thought, let's get it over with.

He started across the room.

"Hey."

He stopped. Angelica Gomez had laid a hand on his arm.

"You got a *cigarillo*?" she asked.

"Sure," Hawes said. He took out his pack and shook one free. Angelica accepted it, hung it on her full lower lip, and waited. Hawes struck a match and lighted the cigarette.

"*Muchas gracias*," she said. "You got good manners. Tha's importan'."

"Yeah," Hawes said, and he started away from the girl, and again she caught his sleeve.

"You know something?"

"What?"

"I hate thees city. You know why?"

"No. Why?"

"No manners. Tha's the troo."

"Well, things are rough all over," Hawes said impatiently.

He started away again, and Angelica said, "Wha's your hurry?" and this time Virginia Dodge turned from the desk and looked at Hawes suspiciously.

"No hurry," he said to Angelica. He could feel Virginia's eyes on his back. Like two relentless drills, they bored at his spinal column.

"So sit down," Angelica said. "Talk to me. Nobody thees city ever have time to talk. Iss diff'ren' on the islan'. On the islan', ever'body got time for everytin.'"

Hawes hesitated. Virginia Dodge was still watching him. Trying to appear unhurried, he pulled up a chair and sat. Casually, perhaps too casually, he shook another cigarette from the package and lighted it. His hand, he noticed, was shaking. He pretended to ignore Virginia completely, pretended to be interested only in the lively company of Angelica Gomez. But as he drew on his cigarette, he was wondering *How long will it be before she remembers she's left a gun in that coat?*

"Where you get that white in your hair?" Angelica asked.

His hand wandered unconsciously to the white smear above his left temple. "I was knifed once," he said. "It grew back this way."

"Where you got knifed?"

"It's a long story."

"I got time."

I haven't, he thought, and then he realized that Virginia was still watching him, and he wondered if she knew he was up to something, and he felt nervousness settle in his stomach like a heavy black brew. He wanted to let out his breath in a giant sigh, wanted to shout something, wanted to pound his fist against the wall. Instead, he forced himself to continue talking in a normal conversational voice, thinking about the pistol all the while, thinking about it so hard he could almost feel his fingers curling around the checked walnut stock.

"I was investigating a burglary," he said. "The woman was pretty hysterical when I got there. I guess she was still in shock. She was terrified when I started to leave. I heard her begin screaming as I was going down the stairwell, the high hysterical screams. I was going to send a patrolman up as soon as I reached the street, but I never got that far. This guy came rushing at me with a knife in his hand."

"This was the burglar?"

"No. No, that's funny part of it. He was the super of the building. He'd heard her screams, and came running upstairs because he thought it was the burglar returning. The hallway was dark and when he saw me he jumped me. And he cut me. I didn't know he was the super, either. I got mad as hell, and I just kept hitting him until he went limp. But he'd already put the gash in my head."

"So what happened?"

"So they shaved the hair off to get at the cut. And when it grew back, it was white. End of story."

"Did the super go to jail?"

"No. He honestly thought I was the burglar."

There was a pause.

"Will I go to jail?"

"Yes. Probably."

There was another pause. He wondered if he should leave now, but Virginia was still watching him. Angelica Gomez sat with her hands folded in her lap. There was sadness on her face, mingled with a hardness that made her seem older than she actually was.

In a thrust at further conversation, Hawes said, "What brought you to the mainland?"

Without hesitation, she answered, "Pan-American Airlines."

"No, no, I meant . . ."

"Oh. You meant . . ." and she burst out laughing, and suddenly there was no hardness to her face. She threw back her head, and the bleached blond hair seemed, for a moment, as natural as her laughter. She was carefree for an instant, all thought of spontaneous mayhem and violent gang retaliation washed from her mind. Her face relaxed, leaving only the natural beauty which was her birthright and which the city could never rob from her. The laughter trailed off. The relaxation dropped from her face like a gossamer veil drifting to the dust. There was only the hardness again, covering the beauty with the glitter of shellac.

"I come here because I am hungry," she said. "Very poor in Puerto Rico." She pronounced the name of the island with Spanish grandeur, rhyming "Puer" with "prayer," discarding the harsh "Porto" of the native mainlander. And, never having been to the island, Hawes listened to her pronunciation of the words and visualized it immediately as a place of rare beauty.

Angelica shrugged. "I get letters from my cousins. Come the city, come the city. So I come. Very easy. The plane fare is loan you, there are people who loan you *dinero*. Later on, you pay them back. With in'ress. So I come. I get here January. Very cold here, I don' expec' thees. I knew would be winter here, but not so cold I don't expec'."

"Where'd you go, Angelica?"

"I go first what they call a hot bed place. You know what thees minns?"

"No. What?"

"It sounds dirtee, but hot bed is not thees. Hot bed is where people come to sleep in shifts, *comprende?* Like they rent the apartment to three diff'ren' people. You come sleep, you leave. Nex' one comes sleep, he leaves Then nex' one comes sleep, he leaves. One apartment, three renns. Very smott, much *dinero* in this For the landlord. Not for the sleeper." She smiled grimly. Hawes smiled with her.

"So," Angelica said, "I stay there awhile 'til all my money is gone, an' then I go live with my cousins for a while. An' then I figure I am become — how you say — burn. Burn. When is too much for someone to carry?"

"Burden," Hawes supplied.

"*Sí*. Burd'n. So I find a man an' go live with him."

"Who?"

119

"Oh, jus' a man. Pretty good man, no police trouble. But I don' live with him now because he beat me once an' thees I don' like. So I leave. An' sometimes I sleep around now, but only when I need bad the money." She paused. "I tell you something."

"What?"

"In Puerto Rico," and again the "Puer" was a prayer, "I am pretty girl. Here, too, I am also pretty — but I am also cheap. You know? I am look at here, an' men think 'I sleep with her.' In Puerto Rico, there is respect. Very diff'ren'."

"How do you mean?"

"In Puerto Rico, a girl walks don the stritt, men look an watch, it is a pretty thing to see. I minn, iss all right a girl could wiggle a little, is nice to see, appreciated. An' also a little comical. I minn, good-natured. Here . . . no. Here, always there is the thinking. 'Cheap. Slut. *Puta.*' I hate thees city."

"Well, you . . ."

"Iss not my fault I don' speak such good English. I learn Spanish. I know *real* Spanish, very high Spanish, very good school Spanish. But Spanish iss no good here. You speak Spanish here, you are a foreigner. But thees is my country, too, no? I am American also, no? Puerto Rico is American, *no es verdad*? But Spanish no good. Spanish here minns *puta*. I hate thees city."

"Angelica . . ."

"You know something? I warm to go back the islan'. I wann to go back there an' never leave. Because I tell you. There I am poor, but there I am me. Angelica Gomez. *Me.* An' there is nobody else the whole worl'

120

who iss also Angelica Gomez. Only me. An' here, I am not me, I am only dirtee Spanish Puerto Rican spic!"

"To *some* people," Hawes said.

Angelica shook her head. "I am in big trouble now, no?" she said.

"Yes. You're in very big trouble."

"*Sí*. So what happens to me now? I go to prison, hah? Maybe worse if thees Kassim dies, hah? An' why do I cut him? You want to know why I cut him? I do it because he forgets one thing. He forgets what everybody else in thees city forgets. He forgets that I am me, Angelica Gomez, an' that what is me is *private* an' nobody can touch unless I say touch. Me. Private." She paused. "Why they cann let a person be private? Goddamn, why they cann leave you alone?"

She seemed suddenly on the verge of tears. He reached out to touch her hand, and she shook her head instantly and violently. He pulled back his fingers.

"I am sorree," she said. "I will not cry. One learns fast in thees city that it does no good to cry, no good at all." She shook her head. "I am sorree. Leave me alone. *Por favor*. Leave me alone. Please. Please."

He rose. Virginia Dodge had turned her attention back to the desk. She sat quite silently, staring at the bottle in front of her. Casually, Hawes walked to the bulletin board near the light switch. Casually, he took a pad from back pocket and began writing into it.

* * *

The boys had got an early start.

It was only 6:25, but the boys had been at it since 3:30 when their last class — a boring lecture in Anthropology

— had let out. This was Friday afternoon and after a hard week of listening to lectures and scribbling down notes, the boys owed it to themselves to throw down a few college-manly drinks.

They had started with beer at the fraternity house across the street from the college. But some stupid frosh pledge had stocked the refrigerator the week before and then forgotten to replenish the dwindling supplies. There were only two dozen cans of beer on ice, and that was barely enough to get the boys under way. And so they'd been forced to leave the intimacy of their private diggings in search of liquid refreshment elsewhere.

They had left the frat house, wearing the uniforms which identified them as true scholars. The uniforms consisted of trousers belted in the back and pleatless in the front and cuffless at the bottom. White button-down shirts topped the trousers. Silk-rep ties curled beneath the collars of the shirts, knotted in the front, fell in slender splendor to the simple punctuation of gold clasps. Dark sports jackets, vented in the rear, with unpadded shoulders, three buttons and sleeves and lapels pressed to roll, man, *roll*, completed the costume. The boys were hatless and coatless. They all wore crewcuts.

By the time they reached the third bar, they were hopelessly crocked.

"One day," Sammy Horn said, "I am going to walk into that rotten Anthropology course and rip off Miss Amaglio's blouse. Then I'm gonna deliver a lecture on the mating habits of the Homo sapiens."

"Who in the world," Bucky Reynolds said, "would ever want to rip off Miss Amaglio's blouse?"

122

"Me, that's who," Sammy said. "And deliver a lecture on the mating . . ."

"All the time, he's got sex on the brain," Jim McQuade said. "Zing, zing, zing, sex, sex, sex."

"Right!" Sammy said emphatically. "Damn right."

"Miss Amaglio," Bucky said, pronouncing the name with great care but nonetheless having a little difficulty with it, "strikes me as being a dried-up old septic tank, and I am surprised — to tell you the truth, Samuel, I am profoundly surprised — that you are harboring dark thoughts of planking her. I am truthfully and profoundly surprised by your lecherous thoughts. Yes."

"Screw you," Sammy said.

"All the time sex on the brain," Jim said.

"I will tell you something," Sammy said, his blue eyes very serious behind his black-rimmed bop spectacles. "Still water runs deep. That is the God's honest truth, I swear to God."

"Miss Amaglio," Bucky said, still having trouble with the name, "is not *still* water, she is *stagnant* water. And I am greatly astounded — astonished, I say — to discover that you, Samuel Horn, could even entertain notions of . . ."

"I am," Sammy admitted.

"That's indecent," Bucky said, ducking his blond crewcut head, and then shaking it mournfully, and then sighing. "Obscene." He sighed again "But, to tell you the truth, I wouldn't mind a little piece of that myself, you know? She has a very foreign sexy-type look, that wench, even though she is about four thousand years old."

Standing at the bulletin board near the light switch, Hawes wrote into his pad aimlessly, waiting for the precise moment of attack. Ideally that moment should be when Virginia Dodge was at the other end of the room. Unfortunately, she showed no signs of moving from the desk behind which she sat in deadly earnestness, staring at the bottle of colorless fluid.

Well then, Hawes thought, the hell with the ideal. Let's just hope she turns her back for a minute, just to give me enough time to snap off the lights.

That's all I need. Just a moment while she turns away, and then the lights go off, and I reach for the gun, left-hand pocket of the coat, mustn't grab for the right- hand pocket by mistake, Jesus, suppose one of the boys thinks there's been a power failure, suppose somebody strikes a match or turns on one of those damn battery- powered emergency lights, is there one in the squadroom? sure, under the kneehole of the junk desk, oh Jesus, don't anybody get any bright ideas, please, pun unintentional, don't anybody throw any light on the subject, pun intentional, don't foul me up by being heroes.

Just let the lights go out, and sit tight, and let me get my mitts on that pistol. Just three seconds. Stick my hand in the pocket, close it around the butt, pull it out, and shove the gun into the side pocket of my pants. That's all I need.

Now if she'd only turn her head.

I'm six inches from the light switch. All she has to do is turn her head, and I make my move.

Come on, Virginia darling, turn that deadly little skull of yours.

"And another visit from downstairs?"

"You can't chance that, Virginia, can you?"

"I can! Because if anyone else comes up, the nitro goes, goddamnit!"

"But what about Carella? You blow us up, and you don't get Carella. You want Carella, don't you?"

"Yes, but . . ."

"Then how can you explode that nitro?"

"How can you chance another gunshot?"

"You can't shoot any of us, can you? It's too risky."

"Get back, she said. "All of you."

"What are you afraid of, Virginia?"

"You've got the gun, not us."

"Can't you fire it?"

"Are you afraid of firing it?"

Hawes came around to the left side of the desk, moving closer to her.

"Get back!" she said.

Willis moved closer on the right, and Virginia whirled thrusting the gun at him. In that instant, Hawes stepped between her and the bottle of nitroglycerin. She was out of the chair in the space of a heartbeat, pushing the chair out from beneath her, and starting to rise. And as she started the rise, Willis — seeing that her hand was away from the bottle, knowing she was off balance as she rose — kicked out with his left foot, swinging it in a backward arc that caught her at the ankles. Hawes shoved at her simultaneously, completing the imbalance, sending Virginia sprawling to the right, toppling toward the floor. She hit the floor with resounding force, and her right hand opened as Hawes scuttled around the desk.

The gun fell from her fingers, slid across the floor, whirled in a series of dizzying circles and then came to a sudden stop.

Willis dove for it.

He extended his hand, and Hawes held his breath because they were getting rid of the crazy bitch at last.

And then Willis shrieked in pain as a three-inch dagger of leather and metal stamped his hand into the floor.

CHAPTER
THIRTEEN

The black skirt was taut over the extended leg of Angelica Gomez. It tightened around a fleshy thigh, pulled back over the knee, ended there in sudden revelation of shapely calf and slender ankle. A black strap circled the ankle and beneath that was a red leather pump with a heel like a stiletto. That heel was buried in the back of Willis' hand.

And then Angelica pulled back her leg and stooped immediately to pick up the gun. From the floor, her skirt pulled back over both knees, her eyes flashing, she whirled on Lieutenant Byrnes, who was reaching for the bottle of nitro on the desk top.

"Don' touch it!" she shouted.

Byrnes stopped cold.

"Away from the desk," she said. "Ever'body! Back! Back!"

They moved from the desk, fanning away from it, backing away from a new menace which seemed more deadly than the first. Angelica Gomez had stabbed a man and, for all they knew, that man might now be dead. She had the law to face, and she also had the street gang to face, and so the look on her face was one of desperate resignation. Angelica Gomez was making her pitch for better or worse, and Christ help whoever stepped into her path.

She rose, the pistol unwavering in her fist.

"I'm ge'n out of here," she said. "Don' nobody try to stop me."

Virginia Dodge was on her feet now. She turned to Angelica, and there was a smile on her face. "Good girl," she said. "Give me the gun."

For a moment, Angelica did not understand. She looked at Virginia curiously and then said, "You crazy? I'm leavin'. Now!"

"I know. Give me the gun. I'll cover them for you. While you go."

"Why I should give you the gun?" Angelica said.

"For Christ's sake, are you on their side? The ones who want to send you to jail? Give me the gun!"

"I don' have to do you no favors. I ask before you let me go, an' you say no. Now you want the gun. You crazy."

"All right, I'll put it in black and white. If you take that gun with you, I'm jumped the minute you leave this room. And that means they'll be on the phone in four seconds and the whole damn police force will be after you. If you give me the gun, I hold them. I keep them here. No phone calls. No radio cars looking for you. You're free."

Angelica thought about this for a moment.

"Give me the gun!" Virginia said, and she took a step closer to Angelica. The Puerto Rican girl stood poised like a tigress, her back arched over into a C, her legs widespread, the gun trembling in her hand. Virginia came closer.

138

"Give it to me," she said.

"You hol' them back?" Angelica asked. "You keep them here?"

"Yes."

"Come then. Come close."

Virginia moved to her side.

"Your hand," Angelica said.

Virginia held out her hand, and Angelica put the gun into it.

"I go now," she said. "You keep them here. I get away. Free," she said, "free."

She started to move. She took one step away from Virginia, her back to the woman. Quickly, Virginia raised the gun. Brutally, she brought it crashing down on the skull of Angelica Gomez. The girl collapsed to the floor, and Virginia stepped over her and moved rapidly to the desk.

"Does anybody still think I'm kidding?" she asked.

Roger, the servant who had been with Jefferson Scott for more than twenty years, was sweeping out the hallway when Carella went upstairs again. Hunched over, a tall thin man with white wisps of hair circling a balding head, he swept up the wooden rectangles, squares, triangles, and splinters of the crowbar's destruction. The foxtail brush worked methodically in thin, precise fingers, sweeping the debris into the dustpan.

"Cleaning up the mess?" Carella asked pleasantly.

"Yes," Roger said. "Yes, sir. Mr. Scott liked things neat."

"How well did you know the old man?" Carella asked.

"I've worked for him a long time, sir," Roger said, rising. "A long time."

"Did you like him?"

"He was a fine man. I liked him very much."

"Did he ever have trouble with any of his sons?"

"Trouble, sir?"

"You know. Arguments. Real quarrels. Any of them ever threaten him?"

"They argued from time to time, sir, but never violently. And never any threats. No, sir."

"Mmm. How about the daughter-in-law? Any trouble when David brought her home?"

"No, sir. Mr. Scott liked her very much. He often said he wished his other sons would do as well when they married."

"I see." Carella paused. "Well, thanks a lot." He paused again. "I want to look over the room another time, see if anything else turns up."

"Yes, sir." Roger seemed reluctant to leave. He stood with the dustpan in one hand and the foxtail in the other seemingly waiting for something.

"Yes?" Carella said.

"Sir, we generally dine at seven. It's past six-thirty now, and I was wondering . . . sir, did you plan to stay for dinner?"

Carella looked at his watch. It was 6:37. "No," he said. "In fact, I'm supposed to be back at the squad by seven. My wife's meeting me there. No, thanks. No dinner." He paused and then, for no earthly reason, said, "We're going to have a baby. My wife is."

"Yes, sir," Roger said. He smiled.

"Yeah," Carella said, and he smiled, too.

In the dimness of the corridor, the two men stood smiling at each other.

"Well," Carella said, "back to work."

"Yes, sir."

Carella went into the room. Outside, he could hear Roger's footsteps padding down the corridor.

So here we are again, folks, he thought. This is Steve Carella coming to you from the intimacy of The Den, where gay night-lifers are dancing to the strains of the Suicide Scott Trio. Vot's dot tune dey're playing, Ludwig? Ah, yes, the "Hangman's Waltz," an old Viennese favorite.

Get a grip, Steve-o, he told himself. You are beginning to lose your marbles. Leave us study this room, and then leave us ask a few more questions and wrap this thing up, yes?

Yes.

The room.

No windows. Assuredly no goddamn windows.

No trapdoors or hidden panels.

Jefferson Scott found hanging there — about ten feet from the entrance doorway, overturned stool at his feet.

Rope thrown over that beam in the ceiling and fastened to the doorknob.

Door opens outward into the corridor.

Scott's weight alone could not have held the door closed.

Hence, door was locked; nor could it be forced open by three heavy men — Christ, these Scotts grow big!

Door could not have been locked from the outside. Required pressure to hold door closed and force to ram bolt across. Hence, no tricky string stuff like they have in detective magazines all the time.

Crowbar action snapped lock from doorjamb, enabled men to force door open, cut down Scott from where he was hanging.

Those are the facts, ma'm.

Now if Joe Friday were here . . .

But he ain't.

There is only me. Steve Carella. And I am good and confused.

Let me see, let me see.

He walked over to the door and studied the bolt hanging loose from one screw. The doorjamb was badly marked; that crowbar had certainly done an excellent job. Old Roger had swept up enough splinters to start a toothpick factory. Carella closed the door. Sure enough the door was weatherstripped, and, sure enough, you had to slam the damn thing and then pull on it hard in order to close it properly. He opened the door out into the corridor again, stepped outside, and closed it behind him. Then he stooped down.

There was a half-inch of space between the bottom of the door and the sill of the room. Carella stuck his fingers under the door. He could feel the metal runner of the weatherstripping, starting about a quarter-inch back from the corridor side of the door. He opened the door again. The weatherstripping lip was set into the door sill, slightly farther back, to catch the runner securely when the door was closed. Again, he closed the door. And again he ran his fingers under the bottom edge, between door and sill. The metal seemed to be dented in one spot, but of course he couldn't be certain. Still, there seemed to be — to the touch at least — a sharp narrow valley at one point. He slid his fingers along the metal, smooth, smooth, smooth, and there! There it was. The sudden small dip.

"Lose something?" the voice behind him said.

Carella turned. Mark Scott was a tall man even if you were standing beside him. When you were crouched on the floor as Carella was, Mark looked enormous. He was as blond as his brother David, broader in the shoulders with the same huge bone structure. His face, in fact despite three covering layers of skin, seemed to have been chiseled from raw bone. He had a flat, hard forehead, and a flat, hard nose. His cheekbones sloped sharply downward to break the otherwise flat regularity of his features. His mouth was full, the lips thick. His eyes were gray, but in the dimness of the corridor, they were almost no-color, almost a colorless opaqueness beneath the bushy blond brows.

Carella got to his feet and dusted off his trouser knees.

"No." he said pleasantly. "I didn't lose anything. But in a sense, I'm trying to find something."

"And what might that be?" Mark said, smiling.

"Oh, I don't know. A way into this room, I suppose."

"Under the door?" Mark asked, the smile still on his mouth. "Have to be awfully thin, don't you think?"

"Sure, sure," Carella said. He opened the door again and stepped into the den. Mark followed behind him.

Carella tapped the hanging slip bolt with his finger, setting it swinging. "I understand this bolt was pretty hard to close," he said. "That right?"

"Yes. One generally had to pull in on the door and then ram the bolt across with all one's strength. I spoke to Father about changing it, but he said it suited him fine. Provided the exercise which was lacking in his life." Mark smiled again. His smile was a charming one, a sudden parting of the thick lips over dazzlingly white teeth.

"Just how hard did you have to pull on the door?" Carella asked.

"I beg your pardon?"

"When slipping the bolt."

"Oh. Very hard."

"Do you imagine your father's weight pulling against the doorknob would have provided the pressure necessary to slip the bolt?"

"To hold the door shut, perhaps yes. But it took quite a bit of pressure to push the bolt across. You are thinking, are you not, of someone having managed it from the outside? With string or something?"

Carella sighed. "Yeah, I was sort of thinking along those lines, yeah."

"Impossible. Ask any of my brothers. Ask Christine. Ask Roger. The lock was impossible. Father should have had it changed, really. We discussed it many times."

"Ever argue about it?"

"With Father? Gracious, no. I made a point of never arguing with him. At least, not after I reached the age of fourteen. I remember making my decision at that time. I made it, as I recall, with a good deal of horror."

144

"The dread Scott decision," Carella said.

"What? Oh. Oh, yes," Mark said, and he smiled. "I decided when I was fourteen that there was no percentage in arguing with Father. Ever since that time, we got along very well."

"Mmm. Right up to now, huh?"

"Yes."

"Who discovered this door was locked, Mr. Scott?"

"Alan did."

"And who went for the crowbar?"

"I did."

"Why?"

"To force the door open. We'd been calling for Father, and he didn't answer."

"And did the crowbar work?"

"Yes. Of course it did."

"Who tried the door after you'd used the crowbar on it?"

"I did."

"And this time it opened?"

"No. There was still Father's weight hanging against it. But we managed to open it a crack — using the crowbar again — and Alan stuck his arm in and cut the rope."

"Did any of you use the crowbar on the *bottom* of the door?" Carella asked.

"The bottom?"

"Yes. Down there. Near the sill."

"Why no. Why would we want to do that?"

"I can't imagine. Are you gainfully employed, Mr. Scott?"

"What?"

"Do you have a job?"

"Well, I . . ."

"Yes or no?"

"I've been training at one of the factories. Preparing for an executive position. Father always felt that executives should learn from the bottom up."

"Did you agree with him?"

"Yes. Of course."

"Where were you . . . ah . . . training?"

"The New Jersey plant."

"For how long?"

"I'd been there for six months."

"How old are you, Mr. Scott?"

"Twenty-seven."

"And what did you do before you went into the New Jersey plant?"

"I was in Italy for several years."

"Doing what?"

"Enjoying myself," Mark said. "When Mother died, she left me a little money. I decided to use it when I got out of college."

"When was that?"

"I was twenty-two when I graduated."

"And you've been in Italy since then?"

"No. The Government interfered with my graduation plans. I was in the Army for two years."

"And then you went to Italy, is that right?"

"Yes."

"You were twenty-four years old at the time?"

"Yes."

"How much money did you have?"

"Mother left me thirty thousand."

"Why'd you come back from Italy?"

"I ran out of money."

"You spent thirty thousand dollars in three years? In *Italy*?"

"Yes, I did."

"That's an awful lot of money to spend in Italy, isn't it?"

"Is it?"

"What I mean is, you must have lived rather grandly."

"I've always lived rather grandly, Mr. Carella," Mark said, and he grinned.

"Mmm. This executive position you were training for. What was it?"

"A sales executive."

"No title?"

"Just a sales executive."

"And what was the salary for the job?"

"Father didn't believe in spoiling his children," Mark said. "He realized that the business his would go to pieces if he simply put his sons in at ridiculously high salaries when they didn't know anything about running the business."

"So what was the starting salary?"

"For that particular job? Fifteen thousand."

"I see. And you live rather grandly. Ran through ten grand a year in Italy. I see."

"That was a *starting* salary, Mr. Carella. Father fully intended Scott Industries to belong to his sons eventually."

"Yes, his will would seem to substantiate that. Did you know about his will, Mr. Scott?"

"All of us did. Father talked of it freely."

"I see."

"Tell me, Mr. Carella," Mark said. "Do you think I killed my own father?"

"Did you, Mr. Scott?"

"No."

"He committed suicide, isn't that right, Mr. Scott?"

"Yes, that's right." Mark Scott paused. "Or do you think I crawled into the room under that crack in the door?"

CHAPTER
FOURTEEN

There she was — the city. All decked out for the pleasures of night, wearing her sleek black satin with a bright red sash. Clusters of jewels hung in her hair, the rectangles of all-night offices blinking at the darkness in defiance of the stars, the shimmering haze in the air over the incredible skyline. A necklace of dazzling light hung from her slender throat, the reds and greens of traffic, the ambers of the street globes, the harsh bright overhead fluorescents of Detavoner Avenue. Her rounded fleshy shoulders rolled to the music of the night, her full breasts heaved ecstatically to the music of the night, mournful music that oozed from the cellar dives of Isola, pounded with the beat of a glittering G-string, music that came with mathematical precision from the cool bop bistros, music that bounced with the cornball rhythms of the supper clubs.

The highways glowed with reflected river light that molded the valleys of her waist, swept North and South over her wide hips, dropped over shapely legs to capture her ankles in neon slave bracelets, terminated in the reflection of pinpoint light glowing from high-heeled slippers on slick wet asphalt.

There she was — the city.

Rushing with the night and the sound of the night, sucking in wild air through parted lips, her eyes glowing bright, bright with the fever of the tempo, Friday night, and the city clasped the weekend to her breasts, held the weekend close in a desperate embrace. A woman was the city, a beautiful woman with life in her loins and treachery in her heart, an exciting woman with a dagger behind her back in long white fingers, a gentle woman who sang forgotten melodies in windswept concrete canyons, a woman of love and a woman of hate, a woman fondled by eight million people who had tasted the pleasures of her body and knew her well and hated her with a deep abiding love.

Eight million people.

Geoffrey Tamblin was a publisher.

He published textbooks. He had been in the racket for thirty-two years, and now — at the age of fifty-seven — he considered himself a knowledgeable guy who knew all the ins and outs of the racket.

Geoffrey Tamblin never called it "the publishing game." To Tamblin, it was "the racket," and he hated it passionately. The thing he particularly despised about the racket was the publishing of books about mathematics. These he detested. His rancor probably went back to a high-school course in Geometry conducted by an old poop named Dr. Fanensel. He was unable to decide, at the age of seventeen, whether he hated Geometry more than Dr. Panensel or vice versa. Now, forty years later, his hatred had grown admirably to include *all* mathematics and *all* teachers and students of mathematics. Plane Geometry, Analytic Geometry, Algebra, Differential Calculus, and even Long and Short Division fell into the sphere of Tamblin's hatred.

And the terrible part of it all was that his firm published a great many mathematics texts. In fact, the largest percentage of his list was devoted to books about mathematics. Which was why Geoffrey Tamblin had three ulcers.

One day, Tamblin thought, I will stop publishing textbooks, and especially mathematics texts. I'll bring out slim volumes of poetry or criticism. Tamblin Books will begin to mean beautiful books. No more "Given X equals 10, and Y equals 12, what then does $\angle$ A equal?" No more "Log C equals Log D, therefore . . ." No more ulcers.

He felt a twinge even thinking about his ulcers.

Poetry, he thought. Slim beautiful volumes of poetry. Ah, that would be wonderful. I'll move to the suburbs and run the firm from there. No more subways. No more rushing. No more schedules. No more crumby editors fresh from Harvard with Phi Beta Kappa keys hanging on their weskits. No more disgruntled artists drawing triangles when they want to be drawing nudes. No more doddering professors bringing their creaky goddamn texts into my office. Only beautiful slim volumes of poetry written by young slim girls with golden hair. Ahhhhhh.

Geoffrey Tamblin lived on Silvermine Road at the outer fringes of the 87th Precinct. Every evening, he walked from his office on Hall Avenue in midtown Isola to the subway a block north. He rode the subway up to

151

Sixteenth, disembarked, and then walked toward his apartment house through a neighborhood which had once been beautiful and quite elite. Now, the neighborhood was going, everything was going, it was the fault of mathematics. The world was reducing everything to simple formulas, there was no reality any more except the reality of mathematics. X times infinity equals a hydrogen explosion. The world would not end in fire — it would end in mathematical symbols.

The neighborhood even smelled bad now. Empty lots strewn with rubble, garbage thrown from windows, street gangs wearing bright silk jackets and committing murder while the policemen slept, gangsters, all gangsters who were more interested in the mathematics of a crossword puzzle than in human decency. I've got to get out of this, poetry, where is all the poetry in the world?

I'll walk past the park tonight, he thought.

The thought excited him. There was a time, before he'd become involved with a world of X's and Y's, when Geoffrey Tamblin could walk the paths of Grover Park and stare up at an orange ball of moon and know with certainty that the city was a place of romance and mystery. Now — with three ulcers — he thought only that he could not walk *through* the park because of potential muggers, he would have to walk *past* it — on Grover Avenue. And still, the thought excited him.

He walked rapidly, thinking of poetry, noticing the mathematical precision of the "green globes hanging outside the police station across the street. 87. Figures. Always figures.

There were three boys walking ahead of him. Juvenile delinquents, gangsters? No, they looked like college boys, potential nuclear physicists, mathematicians. What were they doing up here, all the way uptown? Listen to them sing, Tamblin thought. Did I ever sing? Wait until they come face to face with the unbending reality of plus and minus. Let's hear them sing then, let's hear them . . .

Geoffrey Tamblin broke his stride.

His shoe was sticking to the pavement. Disgustedly he pulled it loose and examined the sole. Chewing gum' Damnit, when would people learn to be clean, throwing gum all over the sidewalk where a man could step on it.

Swearing under his breath, he looked around for a scrap of paper, wishing he had one of Dr. Fanensel's texts to tear up.

He spotted the blue rectangle of paper lying next to the curb, hobbled over to it, and picked it up. He did not even glance at it. It was probably a throwaway from one of the supermarkets, full of this week's specials, prices, prices, figures, figures, where was all the poetry in the world?

Wadding the blue sheet, he rubbed viciously at the gum on his shoe. Then, pure again, he crumpled the paper into a mathematical ball and threw it down the sewer.

It was probably just as well.

Meyer Meyer's message would have made an exceedingly slim volume of poetry.

"'The sun is a-shining to welcome the day,'" sang Sammy, "'and it's hi-ho, come to the fair!'"

"'To the fair, to the fair, to the fair,'" Bucky sang.

"How does the rest go?" Sammy asked.

"'To the fair, to the fair, to the fair,'" Bucky sang.

"Let's sing a college song," Jim said.

"Screw college songs," Sammy said. "Lets sing 'Minnie the Mermaid.'"

"I don't know the words."

"Who needs words? It's emotion that counts, not words."

"Hear, hear," Bucky said.

"Words are only words," Sammy said philosophically, "If they don't come from here. Right here." He tapped his heart.

"Where's this Mason Avenue?" Jim wanted to know. "Where's all these Spanish chicks?"

"Up the street," Sammy said. "North. Don't talk so loud. That's a police station over there."

"I hate cops," Jim said.

"Me, too," Bucky said.

"I've never met a cop," Jim said, "who wasn't an out-and-out son-of-a-bitch."

"Me, too," Bucky said.

"I hate aviators," Sammy said.

"I hate aviators, too," Bucky said. "But I hate cops, too."

"I hate, especially," Sammy said, "jet aviators."

"Oh, especially," Bucky said. "But cops, too."

"Are you still crocked?" Jim asked. "I'm still crocked and it's magnificent. Where are all the Spanish girls?"

"Up the street, up the street, don't get impatient."

"What's that?" Bucky said.

"What's what?"

"That blue piece of paper. Over there."

"What?" Sammy turned to look. "It's a blue piece of paper. What do you think it is?"

"I don't know," Bucky said. "What do you think it is?"

They began walking again, past the second carbon copy of Meyer's message.

"I think it's a letter from a very sad old tart. She uses blue stationery whenever she writes to her imaginary lover."

"Very good," Bucky said. They continued walking.

"What do you think it is?"

"I think it's a birth announcement from a guy who always wanted a boy. Only he got a girl by accident, but all the announcements were already printed on blue."

"Very good," Sammy said. "What do you think it is, Jim?"

"I'm crocked," Jim said.

"Yes, but what do you think it is?"

They continued walking, half a block away from the message now.

"I think it's a blue piece of toilet paper," Jim said.

Bucky stopped walking. "Let's check."

"Huh?"

"Let's see."

"Come on, come on," Jim said "let's not waste time. The *tamales* are waiting."

"Only take a minute," Bucky said, and he turned to go back for the sheet of paper. Jim caught his arm.

"Listen, don't be a nut," Jim said. "Come on."

"He's right," Sammy said. "Who care *what* the damn thing is?"

155

"I do," Bucky said, and he pulled his arm free, whirled, and ran up the street. The other boys watched him as he picked up the sheet of paper.

"Crazy nut," Jim said. "Wasting our time."

"Yeah," Sammy said.

Up the street, Bucky was reading the sheet. Suddenly, he broke into a trot.

"Hey!" he shouted. "Hey!"

Teddy Carella looked at her wrist watch.

It was 6:45.

She walked to the curb, signaled for a cab, and climbed in the moment it stopped.

"Where to, lady?" the cabbie asked.

Teddy took a slip of paper and a pencil from her purse.

Rapidly, she wrote "87th Precinct, Grover Avenue," and handed the slip to the driver.

"Right," he said, and put the taxi in gear.

CHAPTER
FIFTEEN

Alf Miscolo lay in delirium, and in his tortured sleep he cried out, "Mary! Mary!"

His wife's name was Katherine.

He was not a handsome man, Miscolo. He lay on the floor now with his head propped against Willis' jacket. His forehead was drenched with sweat which rolled down the uneven planes of his face. His nose was massive, and his eyebrows were bushy, and there was a thickness about his neck which created the impression of head sitting directly on shoulders. He was not a handsome man, Miscolo, less handsome now in his pain and his delirium. Blood was seeping through the sulfanilamide bandage, and his life was leaking out of his body drop by precious drop, and he cried out again "Mary!" sharply because he once had been in love.

He had been in love a long while ago, and then only for a few short weeks before his ship left Boston. He had never again gone back to that city, never again sought out the girl who'd presented him with a memory that would last a lifetime. His destroyer had been berthed in the Charlestown yards. He was a bosun at the time, the toughest goddamn bosun in the U.S. fleet. The second World War was still a long way off, and Miscolo had only three things on his mind: how to be the toughest goddamn bosun in the U.S. fleet, how to enjoy himself to the fullest, and how to find an Italian meal whenever he left the ship.

He had possibly eaten in every Italian restaurant in Boston before he found the little dive off Scollay Square. Mary worked as a waitress in that dive. Miscolo was twenty-one years old at the time and, to his eyes, Mary was the loveliest creature that walked the face of the earth. He began taking her out. He lived with her for two weeks. In those two weeks, they shared a lifetime together, and then the two weeks were over and the ship pulled out. And Miscolo swam at Waikiki Beach in Honolulu. And he attended a luau on the beach at Kauai, and he ate heikaukau rock crab, and poi and kukui nuts while the hula girls danced. And later, in a Japanese town called Fukuoko — the Japanese were still our friends and no one even dreamt of Pearl Harbor then — Miscolo drank saki with a sloe-eyed girl whose name was Misasan, and he watched her pick up strips of dried fish with chopsticks and later he went to bed with her and learned that Oriental girls do not like to kiss. And on the way back, he hit San Francisco and had a ball there looking down from the hills at the magnificent city spread out in a dazzling array of lights, flushed with his overseas pay, the toughest goddamn bosun in the U.S. fleet.

He never went back to Boston. He met Katherine instead when he was discharged, and he began going steady with her, and he got engaged, and then married, so he never went back to Boston to see the girl named

158

Mary who worked in a sleazy Italian restaurant in Scollay Square.

And now, with his life running red against a Sulfapak, with his body on fire and his head a throbbing black void, he screamed "*Mary!*"

Bert Kling put the wet cloth on Miscolo's forehead.

He was used to death and dying He was a young man, but he had been through the Korean "police action," when death and dying had been a matter of course, an everyday occurrence like waking up to brush your teeth. And he had held the heads of closer friends on his lap, men he knew far better than Miscolo. And yet, hearing the word *Mary* erupt from Miscolo's lips in a hoarse scream, he felt a chill start at the base of his spine rocketing into his brain where it exploded in cold fury. In that moment, he wanted to rush across the room and strangle Virginia Dodge.

In that moment, he wondered whether the liquid in that bottle was really nitroglycerin.

Angelica Gomez sat up and shook her head.

Her skirt was pulled back over her knees, and she propped her elbows on both knees and shook her head again, and then looked around the room with a puzzled expression on her face, like a person waking in a hotel.

And then, of course, she remembered.

She touched the back of her head. A huge knob had risen where Virginia had hit her with the gun. She felt the knob and the area around it, all sensitive to her probing fingers. And as the tentacles of pain spread out from the bruise, she felt with each stab a new rush of outraged anger. She rose from the floor and dusted off

159

her black skirt, and the look she threw at Virginia Dodge could have slain the entire Russian Army.

And in that moment, she wondered whether the liquid in that bottle was really nitroglycerin.

Cotton Hawes touched his cheek where the gun sight has ripped open a flap of flesh. The cheek was raw to the touch. He dabbed at it with a cold wet handkerchief, a cloth no colder than his fury.

And he wondered for the tenth time whether the liquid in that bottle was really nitroglycerin.

Steve Carella, she thought.

I will kill Steve Carella. I will shoot the rotten bastard and watch him die, and they won't touch me because they're afraid of what's in this bottle.

I am doing the right thing.

This is the only thing to do.

There is a simple equation here, she thought: a life for a life.

Carella's life for my Frank's life. And that is justice.

The concept of justice had never truly entered the thoughts of Virginia Dodge before. She had been born Virginia MacCauley, of an Irish mother and a Scotch father. The family had live in Calm's Point at the foot of the famous bridge which joined that part of the city with Isola. Even now, she looked upon the bridge with fond remembrance. She had played in its shadow as a little girl, and the bridge to her had been a wonderous structure leading to all the far corners of the earth. One day, she had dreamt, she would cross that bridge and it would take her to lands brimming with spices and rubies. One day, she would cross that bridge into the sky, and there would be men in turbans, and camels in caravans, and temples glowing with gold leaf.

She had crossed the bridge into the arms of Frank Dodge.

Frank Dodge, to the police, was a punk. He'd been arrested at the age of fourteen for mugging an old man in Grover Park. He'd been considered a juvenile offender by the law, and got off with nothing more serious than a reprimand and a j.d. card. Between the ages of fourteen and seventeen, he'd been pulled in on a series of minor offences — and always his age, his lawyer, and his innocent baby-blue-eyed looks had saved him from incarceration. At nineteen, he committed his first holdup.

This time he was beyond the maximum age limit for a juvenile offender. This time, his innocent baby-blue-eyed looks had lengthened into the severity of near-manhood. This time, they dumped him into the clink on Bailey's Island. Virginia met him shortly after his release.

To Virginia, Frank Dodge was not a punk.

He was the man with the turban astride the long-legged camel, he was the gateway to enchanted lands, rubies trickled from his fingertips, he was her man.

His B-card listed a series of offences as long as Virginia's right arm — but Frank Dodge was her man, and you can't argue with love.

In September of 1953, Frank Dodge held up a gas station. The attendant yelled for help and it happened that a detective named Steve Carella, who was off-duty and driving toward his apartment in Riverhead, heard the calls and drove into the station — but not before Dodge had shot the attendant and blinded him. Carella made the collar. Frank Dodge went to prison — Castleview this time, where nobody played games with thieves. It was discovered, during his first week of imprisonment that Frank Dodge was anything but an ideal prisoner. He caused trouble with keepers and fellow-prisoners alike. He constantly flouted the rules — as archaic as they were. He tried to obtain his release, but each attempt failed. His letters to his wife, read by prison authorities before they left the prison, grew more and more bitter.

In the second year of his term, it was discovered that Frank Dodge was suffering from tuberculosis. He was transferred to the prison hospital. It was in the prison hospital that he had died yesterday.

Today, Virginia Dodge sat with a pistol and a bottle, and she waited for the man who had killed him. In her mind, there was no doubt that Steve Carella was the man responsible for her husband's death. If she had not believed this with all her heart, she'd never have had the courage to come up here with such as audacious plan.

The amazing part of it was that the plan was working so far. They were all afraid of her, actually afraid of her. Their fear gave her great satisfaction. She could not have explained the satisfaction if she'd wanted to, could not have explained her retaliation against all society in the person of Steve Carella, her flouting of the law in such a flamboyant manner. Could she not, in all truth, in all fairness, simply have waited for Carella downstairs and put a bullet in his back when he arrived?

Yes.

In all fairness, she could have. There was no need for a melodramatic declaration of what she was about to do, no need to sit in judgment over the law enforcers as they had sat in judgment over her husband, no need to hold life or death in the palms of her hands, no need to play God to the men who had robbed her of everything she loved.

Or was there a very deep need?

She sat now with her private thoughts. The gun in her hand was steady. The bottle on the table before her caught the slanting rays of the overhead light.

She smiled grimly.

They're wondering, she thought, whether the liquid in the bottle is really nitroglycerin.

"What do you think?" Bucky said.

"I think it's a bunch of crap," Jim said. "Let's go get the Spanish girls."

"Now, wait a minute," Bucky said. "Don't just brush this off. Now just wait a minute."

"Look," Jim said, "you want to play cops and robbers, fine. Go ahead. I don't. I want to go find the Spanish girls. I want to find Mason Avenue. I want to curl up on somebody's big fat bosom. For God's sake, I wanna get laid, for God's sake."

"All right, that can wait. Now suppose this is legit?"

"It isn't," Sammy said flatly.

"Damn right," Jim said.

"How do you know?" Bucky asked.

"In the first place," Sammy said, his eyes bright behind his spectacles, "anybody looking at the thing can see it's a phony right off. 'Detective Division Report'! Now what kind of crap is that?"

"Huh?" Bucky said.

"I mean, Bucky, for crissakes, be sensible. 'Detective Division Report'! Now, you know what this is, men?"

"What?" Bucky said.

"This is a thing, you send away the top of a carton of Chesterfield's to Jack Webb, and he sends you back a bunch of blue sheets together with a Dragnet gun and a whistle so you can keep everybody in the neighborhood up nights."

"It looks legitimate to me," Bucky said.

"It does, huh? Do you see the name of the city anywhere on it? Huh? Tell me that."

"Well, no, but . . ."

"When are you going to grow up, Bucky?" Jim said. "This is the same kind of stuff you get from Buck Rogers. Only his say 'Space Division Report,' and he sends you a disintegrator and a secret decoder."

"What about the message?" Bucky said.

"What about it?" Sammy wanted to know. "Look at it. A woman with a gun and a bottle of nitroglycerin. Boy!"

"What's the matter with that?" Bucky said.

"Completely implausible," Sammy said. "And tell me something. If this crazy dame is sitting there with a gun and a bottle of T.N.T., how in the hell did this Detective Whatever-His-Name-Is manage to type up this note and get it out on the street, huh? Implausible, Bucky. Completely implausible."

"Well, it looks legitimate to me," Bucky said doggedly.

"Look . . ." Jim started. And Sammy interrupted with, "Let me handle this, Jimbo."

"Well, it looks legitimate to me," Bucky said doggedly.

"Is it signed?" Sammy said. "Do you see a signature?"

"Sure," Bucky said. "Detective 2nd/Gr . . ."

"It's typed. But is it *signed?*"

"No."

"So?"

"So what?"

"So, look. You want to stew about this thing all night?"

"No, but. . ."

"What'd we come up here for?"

"Well . . ."

"To play space patrol with Buck Rogers?"

"No, but . . ."

"To waste our time with phony cops and robbers messages typed up by sonic kid on his brother's typewriter?"

"I'm gonna ask you a simple question, man," Sammy said. "Plain and simple. And I want a plain and simple answer, man. Okay?"

"Sure," Bucky said. "But it looks legit . . ."

"Did you come up here to get laid or didn't you?"

"I did."

"Well?"

"Well . . ."

"Come on. Throw that away. Let's get started. The night is young. Huh?" Sammy grinned. "Huh? Come on man. Come on, huh? What do you say? How about it? Huh? Okay?"

Bucky thought it over for a moment.

Then he said, "You go ahead without me. I want to call this number."

"Oh, for the love of holy Buddha!" Sammy said.

The telephone in the squadroom rang at 6:55.

Hal Willis waited for Virginia's signal, and then picked up the receiver.

"Eighty-seventh Squad," he said. "Detective Willis speaking."

"Just a second," the voice on the other end said. The voice retreated from the phone, obviously talking to someone else in the room. "How the hell do I know?" it said. "Turn it over to the Bunco Squad. No, for Christ's sake, what would we be doing with a pickpocket file? Oh, Riley, you're the stupidest sonofabitch I've ever had to work with. I'm on the phone, can you wait just one goddamn minute?" The voice came back onto the line. "Hello?"

"Hello?" Willis said. At the desk opposite him, Virginia Dodge watched and listened.

"Who'm I speaking to?" the voice asked.

"Hal Willis."

"You're a detective, did you say?"

"Yes."

"This the 87th Squad?"

"Yes."

"Yeah. Well then, I guess it's a crank."

"Huh?"

"This is Mike Sullivan down Headquarters. We got a call a little while ago, clocked in at . . . ah . . . just a second . . ." Sullivan rattled some papers on the other end of the line ". . . six forty-nine. Yeah."

"What kind of a call?" Willis said.

"Some college lad. Said he picked up a D.D. report in the street. Had a message typed on it. Something about a broad with a bottle of nitro. Know anything about it?"

At her desk, Virginia Dodge stiffened visibly. The revolver came up close to the neck of the bottle. From where Willis stood, he could see her trembling.

"Nitro?" he said into the phone, and he watched her hand, and he was certain the barrel of the gun would collide with the bottle at any moment.

"Yeah. Nitroglycerin. How about that?"

"No," Willis said. "There's . . . there's nothing like that up here."

"Yeah, that's what I figured. But the kid gave his name and all, so it sounded like it might be a real squeal. Well, that's the way it goes. Thought I'd check anyway, though. No harm in checking, huh?" Sullivan laughed heartily.

"No," Willis said, desperately trying to think of some way to tell Sullivan that the message was real; whoever had sent it, the damn thing was real. "There's certainly no harm checking." He watched Virginia, watched the trembling gun in her hand.

Sullivan continued laughing. "Never know when there'll really be some nut up there with a bomb, huh, Willis?" Sullivan said, and he burst into louder laughter.

"No, you . . . you never know," Willis said.

"Sure." Sullivan's laughter trailed off. "Incidentally, is there a cop up there by the name of Meyer?"

Willis hesitated. Had Meyer sent the message? Was it signed? If he said "Yes," would that be the end of it, and would Sullivan make the connection? If he said "No," would Sullivan investigate further, check to see which cops manned the 87th. And would Meyer . . .

"You with me?" Sullivan asked.

"What? Oh, yes."

"Answer him!" Virginia whispered.

"We sometimes get a lousy connection," Sullivan said, "I thought maybe we'd got cut off."

"No, I'm still here," Willis said.

"Yeah. Well, how about it. Any Meyer there?"

"Yes. We have a Meyer."

"Second grade?"

"Yes."

"That's funny," Sullivan said. "This kid said the note was signed by a second grade named Meyer. That's funny, all right."

"Yes," Willis said.

"And you got a Meyer up there, huh?"

"Yes."

"Boy, that sure is funny," Sullivan said. "Well, no harm in checking, huh? What? For God sake's, Riley, can't you see I'm on the phone? I gotta go, Willis. Take it easy, huh? Nice talking to you."

And he hung up.

Willis put the phone back into the cradle.

Virginia Dodge put down her receiver, picked up the bottle of nitro and slowly walked to where Meyer Meyer was sitting at the desk near the window.

She did not say a word.

She put the bottle down on the desk before him and then she brought her arm across her body and swung the gun in a backhanded swipe which ripped open Meyer's lip. Meyer put up his hands to cover his face, and again the gun came across, again, again, numbing his wrists, forcing his hands down until there was only the vicious metal swiping at his eyes and his bald head and his nose and his mouth.

Virginia's eyes were bright and hard.

Viciously, cruelly, brutally, she kept the pistol going like a whipsaw until, bleeding and dazed, Meyer Meyer collapsed on the desk top, almost overturning the bottle of nitroglycerin.

She picked up the bottle and looked at Meyer coldly.

Then she walked back to her own desk.

CHAPTER
SIXTEEN

"I hated the old bastard and I'm glad he's dead," Alan Scott said.

He seemed to have lost all the shocked timidity with which he'd greeted Carella yesterday. They stood in the gun room of the old house, on the main floor, a room lined with heads and horns. A particularly vicious looking tiger head hung on the wall behind Alan, and the expression on his face now — as contrasted to his paleness yesterday — seemed to match that of the tiger.

"That's a pretty strong admission to make, Mr. Scott," Carella said.

"Is it? He was a vicious mean bastard. He's ruined more men with his Scott Industries, Inc., than I can count on both hands. Was I supposed to have loved him? Did you ever grow up with a tycoon?"

"No," Carella said. "I grew up with an Italian immigrant who was a baker."

"You haven't missed anything, believe me. The old bastard's power wasn't quite absolute, but he had enough to make him almost absolutely corrupt. As far as I'm concerned he was a big chancre dripping corruption. My father. Dear old dad. A murdering son of a bitch."

"You seemed pretty upset by his death yesterday."

"Only by the facts of death Death is always shocking. But there was no love for him, believe me."

"Did you hate him enough to kill him, Mr. Scott?"

"Yes. Enough to kill him. But I didn't. Not that I probably wouldn't have sooner or later. But I didn't do *this* job. And that's why I'm willing to level with you. I'll be damned if I'm going to get involved in something I had nothing to do with. You *do* suspect murder, don't you? That's why you're hanging around so long, isn't it?"

"Well . . ."

"Come on, Mr. Carella, let's play it straight with each other. You know the old bastard was killed."

"I know nothing for sure," Carella said. "He was found in a locked room, Mr. Scott. In all truth, it looks pretty much like suicide."

"Sure. But we know it isn't, don't we? There are a lot of clever people in this rotten family who can do tricks that'd make Houdini look sick. Don't let the locked room throw you. If somebody wanted him dead badly enough, that person would find a way of doing it. And making it *look* like suicide."

"Who, for example?"

"Me, for example," Alan said. "If I'd ever decided to really kill him, I'd work it out, don't worry. Somebody just beat me to it, that's all."

"Who?" Carella said.

"You want suspects? We've got a whole family full of them."

"Mark?"

"Sure. Why not Mark? He's been pushed around by the old bastard all his life. He hasn't said a word against him since the time he was fourteen. All that hatred building up inside while he smiled on the outside. And the latest slap in the face, sending Mark to that New Jersey rattrap where — when he finishes his cheap on-the-job-training — he goes into the firm at the magnificent salary of fifteen thousand dollars a year. For the boss's son! Why, the old bastard pays his file clerks more."

"You're exaggerating," Carella said.

"All right, I'm exaggerating. But don't think Mark liked what the old bastard was doing to him. He didn't like it one damn bit. And David had his own reasons for killing dear father."

"Like what?"

"Like lovely Christine."

"What are you saying, Mr. Scott?"

"What does it sound like I'm saying?"

"You mean . . ."

"Sure. Look, I'm playing this straight with you, Carella. My hate is big enough to share, believe me. And I don't want to see my neck stretched for something somebody else did, even if he deserved it."

"Then your father . . ."

"My father was a lecherous old toad who kept Christine in this house by threatening to cut David off penniless if they left. Period. Not nice, but there it is."

"Not nice at all. And Christine?"

"Try talking to her. An iceberg. Maybe she liked the setup, how do I know? At any rate, she knew who buttered her bread. And it was well-buttered, believe me."

"Maybe you all got together, Mr. Scott, to do the job. Is that a possibility?"

"This family couldn't get together to start a bridge game," Alan said. "It's a wonder we managed to open that door in concert. You've heard of togetherness? This family's motto is 'apartheid' Maybe it'll be different now that he's dead — but I doubt it."

"Then you believe that someone in this house — one of your brothers, or Christine — killed your father?"

"Yeah. That's what I believe."

"Through a locked door?"

"Through a locked bank vault, if you will, with six inches of lead on every damn wall. Where there's a will there's a way."

"And there was a fat will here," Carella said.

Alan Scot did not smile. "I'll tell you something, Detective Carella. If you work this from the motive angle, you'll go nuts. We've got enough motive in this run-down mansion to blow up the entire city."

"How then, Mr. Scott, would you suggest that I work it?"

"I'd find out how somebody managed to hang the bastard through a locked door. Figure out *how* it was done, and you'll also figure out who did it. That's my guess, Mr Carella."

"And, of course," Carella said, "that's the easiest part of detective work. Everyone knows that."

Alan Scott did not smile

"I'm leaving," Carella said. "There isn't much more I can do here tonight."

"Will you be back tomorrow?"

"Maybe. If I think of anything."

"Otherwise?"

"Otherwise it's a suicide. We've got motive, as you say, plenty of it. And we've got means. But, man, we sure are lacking in the opportunity department. I'm no genius, Mr. Scott. I'm just a working stiff. If we still suspect a homicide, we'll dump the case in the Open File." Carella shrugged.

"You didn't strike me as being that kind of a man, Mr. Carella," Alan said.

"Which kind of a man?"

"The kind who gives up easily."

Carella stared at him for a long moment. "Don't confuse the Open File with the Dead Letter department of the Post Office," he said at last. "Good night, Mr. Scott."

When Teddy Carella walked into the squadroom at two minutes past seven, Peter Byrnes thought he would have a heart attack. He saw her coming down the corridor and at first he couldn't believe he was seeing correctly and then he recognized the trim figure and proud walk of Steve's wife, and he walked quickly to the railing.

"What are you doing?" Virginia said.

"Somebody coming," Byrnes answered, and he waited. He did not want Virginia to know this was Carella's wife. He had watched the woman grow increasingly more tense and jumpy since the pistol whipping of Meyer, and he did not know what action she might conceivably take against Teddy were she to realize her identity. In the corner of the room, he could

174

see Hawes administering to Meyer. Badly cut, Meyer tried to peer out of his swollen eyes. His lip hung loose, split down the center by the unyielding steel of the revolver. Hawes, working patiently with iodine, kept mumbling over and over again, "Easy, Meyer, easy," and there was a deadly control to his voice as if he — as much as the nitro — were ready to explode into the squadroom.

"Yes, Miss?" Byrnes said.

Teddy stopped dead outside the railing, a surprised look on her face. If she had read the lieutenant's lips correctly . . .

"Can I help you, Miss?" he said

Teddy blinked.

"Get in here, you," Virginia barked from her desk. Teddy could not see the woman from where she stood. And, not seeing her, she could not "hear" her. She waited now for Byrnes to spring the punch line of whatever gag he was playing, but his face remained set and serious, and then he said, "Won't you come in, Miss?" and — puzzled even more now — Teddy entered the squadroom.

She saw Virginia Dodge immediately and knew intuitively that Byrnes was trying to protect her.

"Sit down," Virginia said. "Do as I tell you and you won't get hurt. What do you want here?"

Teddy did not, could not answer.

"Did you hear me? What are you doing here?"

Teddy shook her head helplessly.

"What's the matter with her?" Virginia asked impatiently. "Damnit, answer me."

"Don't be frightened, Miss," Byrnes said. "Nothing will happen to you if . . ." He stopped dead, feigning discovery, and then turned to Virginia "I think . . . I think she's a deaf mute," he said.

"Come here," Virginia said, and Teddy walked to her. Their eyes locked over the desk. "Can you hear?"

Teddy touched her lips.

"You can read my lips?"

Teddy nodded.

"But you can't speak?"

Teddy shook her head.

Virginia shoved a sheet of paper across the desk. She took a pencil from the tray and tossed it to Teddy. "There's paper and pencil. Write down what you want here."

In a quick hand, Teddy wrote "Burglary" on the sheet and handed it to Virginia.

"Mmm," Virginia said. "Well, you're getting a lot more than you're bargaining for, honey. Sit down." She turned to Byrnes and, in the first kind words she'd uttered since coming into the squadroom, she said, "She's a pretty little thing, isn't she?"

Teddy sat.

"What's your name?" Virginia asked. "Come over here and write down your name."

Byrnes almost leaped forward to intercept Teddy as she walked to the desk again. Teddy picked up the pencil and rapidly wrote "Marcia . . ." She hesitated. A last name would not come. In desperation, she finally wrote her maiden name — "Franklin."

176

"Marcia Franklin," Virginia said. "Pretty name. You're a pretty girl, Marcia, do you know that? Can you read my lips?"

Teddy nodded.

"Do you know what I'm saying?"

Again, Teddy nodded.

"You're very pretty. Don't worry, I won't hurt you. I'm only after one person, and I won't hurt anybody unless they try to stop me. Have you ever loved anyone, Marcia?"

Yes, Teddy said with her head.

"Then you know what it's like. Being in love. Well, someone killed the man I loved, Marcia. And now I'm going to kill him. Wouldn't you do that, too?"

Teddy stood motionless.

"You would. I know you would. You're very pretty, Marcia. I was pretty once — until they took my man away from me. A woman needs a man. Life's no good without a man. And mine is dead. And I'm going to kill the man who's responsible. I'm going to kill a rotten bastard named Steve Carella."

The words hit Teddy with the force of a pitched baseball. She flinched visibly, and then she caught her lips between her teeth, and Virginia watched her in puzzlement and then said, "I'm sorry, honey, I didn't mean to swear. But I . . . this has been . . ." She shook her head.

Teddy had gone pale. She stood with her lip caught between her teeth, and she bit it hard, and she looked at the revolver in the hand of the woman at the desk, and her first impulse was to fling herself at the gun. She looked at the wall clock. It was 7:08. She turned toward Virginia and took a step forward.

"Miss," Byrnes said, "that's a bottle of nitroglycerin on the desk there." He paused. "What I mean is, any sudden movement might set it off. And hurt a lot of people."

Their eyes met. Teddy nodded.

She turned away from Virginia and Byrnes, crossing to sit in the chair facing the slatted railing, hoping the lieutenant had not seen the sudden tears in her eyes.

CHAPTER
SEVENTEEN

The clock read 7:10.

Teddy thought only, *I must warn him.*

Methodically, mechanically, the clock chewed time, swallowed it, spat digested seconds into the room. The clock was an old one, and its mechanism was audible to everyone but Teddy, *whirr, whirr,* and the old clock digested second after second until they piled into minutes and the hands moved with a sudden click in the stillness of the room.

7:11 . . .

7:12 . . .

I must warn him, she thought. She had given up the thought of jumping Virginia and thought only of warning Steve now. I can see the length of the corridor from here, she thought, can see the top step of the metal stairway leading from below. If I could hear I would recognize his tread even before he came into view because I know his walk, I have imagined the sound of his walk a thousand times. A masculine sound, but lightfooted, he moves with animal grace, I would recognize the sound of his walk the moment he entered the building — if only I could hear.

But I cannot hear, and I cannot speak. I cannot shout a warning to him when he enters this second floor corridor. I can only run to him. She will not use the nitro, not if she knows Steve is in the building where she can shoot him. She needs the nitro for her escape. So I'll run to him and be his shield, *he must not die.*

And the baby?

The baby, she thought. Hardly a baby yet, a life just begun, but Steve must not die. Myself, yes. The baby, yes. But not Steve. I will run to him. The moment I see him, I will run to him, and then let her shoot. But not Steve.

She had almost lost him once, she could remember that Christmas as if it were yesterday, the painfully white hospital room, and her man gasping for breath. She had hated his occupation then, detested police work and criminals, abhorred the chance circumstances which had allowed her husband to be shot by a narcotics peddler in a city park. And then she had allowed her hatred to dissolve, and she had prayed, simply and sincerely, and all the while she knew that he would die and that her silent world would truly become silent. With Steve, there was no silence. With Steve, she was surrounded by the noise of life.

This was not a time for prayer.

All the prayers in the world would not save Steve now.

When he comes, she thought, I will run to him and I will take the bullet.

When he comes . . .

The clock read 7:13.

That isn't nitroglycerin, Hawes thought.

Maybe it is.

That isn't nitroglycerin.

It can't be. She handles it like water, she treats it with all the disdain she'd give to water, she wouldn't be so damn careless with it if it were capable of exploding.

It isn't nitroglycerin.

Now wait a minute, he told himself, let's just wait a minute, let's not rationalize a desire into a fact.

I want desperately for the liquid in that bottle to be water. I want it because for the first time in my life I am ready to knock a woman silly. I am ready to cross this room and, gun be damned, knock her flat on her ass and keep hitting her until she is senseless. That is the way I feel right now, and chivalry can go to Hell because that is the way I feel. I know it's not particularly nice to go around slugging women, but Virginia Dodge has become something less than a woman, or perhaps something more than a woman, she has become something inhuman and I no more consider her a woman than I would apply gender to a telephone or a pair of shoes.

She is Virginia Dodge.

And I hate her.

And I'm ashamed because I hate so goddamn deeply. I did not think myself capable of such hatred, but she has brought it out in me, she has enabled me to hate deeply and viciously. I hate her, and I hate myself for hating, and this causes me to hate deeper. Virginia Dodge has reduced me to an animal, a blind animal responding to a pain that is being inflicted. And the curious thing is that the pain is not my own. Oh, the cheek, I've been hit harder before, the cheek doesn't matter. But what she did to Miscolo, and what she did to that Puerto Rican girl, and what she did to Meyer, these are things I cannot excuse, rationally or emotionally. These are pains inflicted on humans who have never done a blessed solitary thing to the non-human called Virginia Dodge. They were simply here and, being here, she used them, she somehow reduced them to meaningless ciphers.

And this is why I hate.

I hate because I . . . I and every other man in this room . . . have allowed her to reduce humans to ciphers. She has robbed them of humanity, and by allowing her to rob one man of humanity, by allowing her to strip a single human being of all his godly dignity, I have allowed her to reduce *all* men to a pile of rubbish.

So here I am, Virginia Dodge.

Cotton Hawes is my name, and I am a one-hundred-percent white Protestant American raised by God-fearing parents who instilled in me a sense of right and wrong, and who taught me that women are to be treated with courtesy and chivalry — and you have turned me into a jungle animal ready to kill you, hating you for what you've done, ready to kill you.

The liquid in that bottle is *not* nitroglycerin.

This is what I believe, Virginia Dodge.

Or at least, this is what I am on the road to believing. I do not yet fully believe it. I'm working on it, Virginia. I'm working on it damn hard.

I don't have to work on the hatred. The hatred is there, and it's building all the time and God help you, Virginia Dodge, when I'm convinced, when I've convinced myself that your bottle of nitroglycerin is a big phony.

God help you, Virginia, because I'll kill you.

The answer came to him all at once.

Sometimes it comes that way.

He had left Alan Scott in the old mansion, had walked through the stillness of a house gone silent with death, into the huge entry hall with its cut-glass chandelier and its ornate mirror. He had taken his hat from the marble topped table set in front of the mirror, wondering why he'd worn the hat, he very rarely wore a hat, and then realizing that he had not worn a hat yesterday, and then further realizing that the power of the rich is an intimidating one.

We mustn't be intolerant, he thought. We mustn't blame the very rich for never having experienced the sheer ecstasy of poverty.

Smiling grimly, he had faced the mirror, set his hat on his head, and then opened the huge oak door leading outside. Darkness covered the property. A single light burned at the far end of the walk. There was the smell of woodsmoke on the air.

He had started down the path, thinking of October, and woodsmoke, and burning leaves, and musing about this bit of Exurbia in the center of the city. How nice to be exurban, how nice to burn leaves. He glanced over his shoulder, toward the garage. A figure was silhouetted there against the star-filled sky, a giant of a man, one of the brothers, no doubt, the smoke from the small fire trailing up past his huge body. One of the magnificent Scotts burning leaves, you'd think a job like that would be left to Roger, or the caretaker, no caretaker for the Scott estate? Tch, tch, no caretaker to burn the . . .

It came to him then.

Woodsmoke.

Wood.

And one of the brothers burning his own fire.

Wood. Wood! For Cnrist's sake, wood, of course, of course!

He turned suddenly and started back up the path to the garage.

How do you lock a door? he thought, and his thoughts mushroomed onto his face until he was grinning like an absolute idiot. How do you lock it from the outside and let it seem it's been locked from the inside?

To begin with, you rip the slip bolt from the doorjamb, so that when the door is finally forced open, it looks as if the lock was snapped in the process. That's the first thing you do, and by Christ, that explains all the marks on the *inside* of the room, how the hell could the crowbar have got that far inside, why weren't you thinking, Carella, you moron?

So first you snap the lock.

You have already strangled the old man, and he is lying on the floor while you work on the slip bolt, carefully prying it loose so that it hangs from one screw, so that it will look very realistically snapped when the door is later forced.

Then you put a rope around the old man's neck, and you toss one end of it over the beam in the ceiling, and you pull him up so that he's several feet off the ground. He's a heavy man, but so are you, and you're working with extra adrenalin shooting through your body, and all you have to do is get him off the floor several feet. And then you back away toward the door and tie the rope around the doorknob.

184

The old man is dangling free at the other end of the room.

You shove on the door now. This isn't too difficult. It only has to open wide enough to permit you to slip out of the room. And now you're out, and the old man's weight pulls the door shut again. The slip bolt, on the inside, is dangling loose from one screw.

And you are in the corridor, and the problem now is how to give the appearance of the door being locked so that you and your brothers can tug on it to no avail.

And how do you solve the problem?

By using one of the oldest mechanical devices known to mankind.

And who?

It had to be, it couldn't be anyone else but the first person to try the door after the crowbar was used on it, the first person to step close enough to . . .

"Who's there?" the voice said.

"Mark Scott?" Carella said.

"Yes? Who's that?"

"Me. Carella."

Mark stepped closer to the small fire. The smoke drifted up past his face. The flames, dwindling now, threw a flickering light onto his large features.

"I thought you'd gone long ago," he said. He held a rake in his hands, and he poked at the embers with it now so that the fire leaped up in renewed life, tinting his face with a yellow glow.

"No, I'm still here."

"What do you want?" Mark said.

"You," Carella said simply

"I don't understand."

"I'm taking you with me, Mark," Carella said

"What for?"

"For the murder of your father."

"Don't be ridiculous," Mark said.

"I'm being very sensible," Carella said. "Did you burn it?"

"Burn what? What are you talking about?"

"I'm talking about the way you locked that door from the outside."

"There's no outside lock on that door," Mark said calmly.

"What you used was just as effective as a lock. And the more a person tugged against it, the more effective it became, the tighter it locked that door."

"What are you talking about?" Mark said.

"I'm talking about a wedge," Carella said, "a simple triangle of wood. A wedge . . ."

"I don't know what you mean," Mark said

"You know what I mean, damnit. A wedge, a simple triangular piece of wood which you kicked under the door narrow end first. Any outward pressure on the door only pulled it toward the wide end of the triangle, tightening it."

"You're crazy," Mark said. "We had to use a crowbar on that door. It was locked from the inside. It . . ."

"It was held closed by your wooden wedge which, incidentally, put a dent in the weatherstripping under the door. The crowbar only splintered a lot of wood which fell to the floor. Then you stepped up to the door. *You,* Mark. You stepped up to it and fumbled with the doorknob and — in the process — kicked out the wedge so that the door, for all intents and purposes, was now unlocked. And then, of course, you and your brothers were able to pull it open, despite your father's weight hanging against . . ."

"This is ridiculous," Mark said. "Where'd you . . ."

"I saw Roger sweeping up the debris in the hallway. The splintered wood, *and* your wedge. A good camouflage, that splintered wood. That's what you're burning now, isn't it? The wood? *And* the wedge?"

Mark Scott did not answer. He began moving even before Carella had finished his sentence. He swung the rake back over his shoulder and then let loose with it as if he were swinging a baseball bat, catching Carella completely by surprise. The blow struck him on the side of the neck, three of the rake's teeth entering the flesh and drawing blood. Mark pulled the rake back again. Carella, dizzy, stepped forward with his hands outstretched, and again the rake fell, this time on the forearm of Carella's outstretched right arm.

His arm dropped, numb. He tried to lift it, tried to reach for the Police Special in his right hip pocket, but the arm dangled foolishly, and he cursed its inability to move and then noticed that the rake was back again, ready for another swing, and he knew that this swing would do it, this swing would knock his head clear into the River Harb.

He lunged forward, inside the swing, as the rake cut the air. He grasped with his left hand, reaching for a grip on Mark's clothing, catching the tie knotted loosely around his throat. Mark, off balance from his swing, pulled back instantly, and Carella moved forward with the movement of the bigger man, shoving him backward, and then suddenly tugging forward again on the tie.

Mark fell.

He dropped the rake and spread his hands out to cushion the fall, and Carella went down with him, knowing he must not come into contact with the bigger man's hands — hand which had already strangled once.

Silently, grotesquely, they rolled on the ground toward the fire, Mark struggling for a grip at Carella's throat, Carella holding to the tie as if it were a hangman's noose. They rolled over the fire, scattering sparks onto the lawn, almost extinguishing it. And then Carella dropped the tie, and leaped to his feet and, his right hand useless, his left lacking any real power, brought his foot back and released it in a kick that caught Mark on the left shoulder, spinning him back to the ground.

Carella closed in.

Again he kicked, and again, using his feet with the precision of a boxer. And then, backing off, he reached behind him with his left hand in a curious inverted draw, and faced Mark Scott with the .38 in his fist.

"Okay, get up," he said.

"I hated him," Mark said. "I've hated him ever since I was old enough to walk. I've wanted him dead ever since I was fourteen."

"You got what you wanted," Carella said. "Get up."

Mark got to his feet. "Where are we going?" he asked.

"Back to the squad," Carella said. "It'll be a little more peaceful there."

CHAPTER
EIGHTEEN

"Where is he?" Virginia Dodge said impatiently. She looked up at the clock. "It's almost seven-thirty. Isn't he supposed to report back here?"

"Yes," Byrnes said.

"Then where the hell is he?" She slammed her left fist down on the desk top. Hawes watched. The bottle of nitro, jarred, did not explode.

It's water, Hawes thought. Goddamnit, it's *water!*

"Have you ever had to wait for anything, Marcia?" Virginia said to Teddy. "I feel as if I've been in this squadroom all my life."

Teddy watched the woman, expressionless.

"You ro'n bitch," Angelica Gomez said. "You should wait in *Hell*, you dirtee bitch."

"She's angry," Virginia said, smiling. "The Spanish onion is angry. Take it easy, Chiquita. Just think, your name'll be in the newspapers tomorrow."

"An' your name, too," Angelica said. "An' maybe it be in the *dead* columns."

"I doubt that," Virginia said, and all humor left her face and her eyes. "The newspapers will . . ." She stopped. "The newspapers," she said, and this time she said the words with the tone of discovery. Hawes watched the discovery claim her face, watched as she stirred her memory. Her eyes were beginning to narrow.

"I remember reading a story about Carella," she said. "In one of the newspapers. The time he got shot. It mentioned that his wife . . ." She paused. "His wife was a deaf mute!" she said, and she turned glaring eyes on Teddy. "What about it, Marcia Franklin? What about it?"

Teddy did not move.

"What are you doing here?" Virginia said. She had begun rising.

Teddy shook her head.

"Are you Marcia Franklin, come to report a burglary? Or are you Mrs. Steve Carella? Which? Answer me!"

Again Teddy shook her head.

Virginia was standing now, her attention riveted to Teddy. Slowly, she came around the desk, sliding along its edge, ignoring the bottle on its top completely. It was as if, having found someone she believed to be related to Carella, her wait was nearing an end. It was as if — should this woman be Carella's wife — she could now tnily begin to vent her spleen. Her decision showed on her face. The hours of waiting, the impatience of the ordeal, the necessity for having to deal with other people while her real quarry delayed his entrance showed in the gleam of her eyes and the hard set of her mouth. As she approached Teddy Carella, Hawes knew instinctively that she would inflict upon her the same — if not worse — punishment that Meyer Meyer had suffered.

"Answer me!" Virginia screamed, and she left the desk completely now, the bottle of nitro behind her, advanced to Teddy, and stood before her, a dark solemn judge and iury.

She snatched Teddy's purse from her arm, and snapped it open. Byrnes, Kling, Willis, stood to the right of Teddy, near the coat rack. Miscolo was unconscious on the floor behind Virginia, near the filing cabinets. Only Meyer and Hawes were to her right and slightly behind her — and Meyer was limp, his head resting on his folded arms.

Quickly, deftly, Virginia rifled through the purse. She found what she was looking for almost immediately. Immediately, she read it aloud.

"Mrs. Stephen Carella, 837 Dartmouth Road, Riverhead. In case of emergency, call . . ." She stopped. "Mrs Stephen Carella," she said. "Well, well, Mrs. Stephen Carella." She took a step closer to Teddy, and Hawes watched, hatred boiling inside him, and he thought, *It isn't nitro, it isn't nitro, it isn't nitro . . .*

"Aren't you the pretty one, though?" Virginia said. "Aren't you the well-fed, well-groomed beauty? You've had your man, haven't you? You've had your man, and you've still got your good looks, haven't you? Pretty, you bitch, look at me! LOOK AT ME!"

I'll jump her, Teddy thought. Now. While she's away from the nitro. I'll jump her now, and she'll fire, and the rest will grab her, and it will be all over. Now. Now.

But she did not jump.

Hypnotized as if by a snake, she watched the naked hatred on Virginia Dodge's face.

"I was pretty once," Virginia said, "before they sent Frank away. Do you know how old I am? I'm thirty-two. That's young. That's young, and I look like a hag, don't I, like death one of them said. Me, me, I look like death because your husband robbed me of *my* Frank. *Your* husband, you bitch. Oh, I could rip that face of yours apartl I could rip it, rip it for what he's done to me! Do you hear me, you little bitch!"

She stepped closer, and Hawes knew the gun would flash upward in the next moment.

He told himself for the last time, *There's no nitro in that bottle*, and then he shouted, "Hold it!"

Virginia Dodge turned to face him, moving closer to the desk and the bottle on it, blocking Byrnes and the others from it.

"Get away from her," Hawes said.

"What!" Virginia's tone was one of complete disbelief.

"You heard me. Get away from her. Don't lay a hand on her."

"Are you giving me orders?"

"Yes!" Hawes shouted. "Yes, I am giving you orders! Now how about that, Mrs. Dodge? How about it? *I* am giving *you* orders! One of the crawly little humans is daring to give God orders. Keep away from that girl. You touch her and . . ."

"And what?" Virginia said. There was a sneer in her voice, supreme confidence in her stance — but the gun in her hand was trembling violently.

"I'll kill you, Mrs. Dodge," Hawes said quietly. "That's what, Mrs. Dodge. I'll kill you."

He took a step toward her.

"Stand where you are!" Virgnia yelled.

"No, Mrs. Dodge," Hawes said. "You know something? I'm not afraid of your wedge any more, your little bottle. You know why? Because there's nothing but water in it, Mrs. Dodge, and I'm not afraid of water. I *drink* water! By the gallon, I drink it!"

"Cotton," Byrnes said, "don't be a . . ."

"Don't take another step!" Virginia said desperately, the gun shaking.

"Why not? You going to shoot me? Okay, damnit, shoot me! But shoot me a lot because one bullet isn't going to do it! Shoot me twice and then keep shooting me because I'm coming right at you, Mrs. Dodge, and I'm going to take that gun away from you with any strength that's left in my hands, and I'm going to stuff it right down your throat! I'm coming, Mrs. Dodge, you hear me?"

"Stop! Stop where you are!" she screamed. "The nitro . . ."

"There *is* no nitro!" Hawes said, and he began his advance in earnest, and Virginia turned to face him fully now. To her left, Byrnes gestured to Teddy, who began moving slowly toward the men who stood just inside the gate. Virginia did not seem to notice. Her hand was shaking erratically as she watched Hawes.

"I'm coming, Mrs. Dodge," Hawes said, "so you'd better shoot now if you're going to because . . ."

And Virginia fired.

The shot stopped Hawes. But only momentarily, and only in the way any sudden sharp noise will stop anyone. Because the bullet had missed him by a mile, and he began his advance again, moving across the room toward her, watching Byrnes slip Teddy past the railing and practically shove her down the corridor. The others did not move. Shut off from the bottle of nitro, they nonetheless stood rooted in the room, facing an imminent explosion.

"What's the matter?" Hawes said. "Too nervous to shoot straight? Your hand trembling too much?"

Virginia backed toward the desk. This time, he *knew* she was going to fire. He sidestepped an instant before she squeezed the trigger, and again the slug missed him, and he grinned and shouted, "That does it, Mrs. Dodge! You'll have every cop in the city up here now!"

"The nitro . . ." she said, backing toward the desk.

"What nitro? There *is* no nitro!"

"I'll knock it to the . . ."

And Hawes leaped.

The gun went off as he jumped, and this time he heard the rushing *whoosh* of the bullet as it tore past his head, missing him. He caught at Virginia's right hand as she swung it toward the desk and the bottle of nitroglycerin. He clung to her wrist tightly because there was animal strength in her arm as she flailed wildly at the bottle, reaching for it.

He pulled her arm up over her head and then slammed it down on the desk top, trying to knock the gun loose, and the bottle slid towards the edge of the desk.

194

He slammed her hand down again, and again the bottle moved, closer to the edge as Virginia's fingers opened and the gun dropped to the floor.

And then she twisted violently in his arms and flung herself headlong across the desk in a last desperate lunge at the bottle standing not two inches from its edge. She slipped through his grip, and he caught at her waist and then yanked her back with all the power of his shoulders and arms, pulling her upright off the desk, and then clenching his fist into the front of her dress, and drawing his free hand back for a blow that would have broken her neck.

His hand hesitated in mid-air.

And then he lowered it, unable to hit her. He shoved her across the room and said only, "You bitch!" and then stooped to pick up the gun.

Meyer Meyer lifted his battered head. "What . . . what happened?" he said.

"It's over," Hawes answered.

Byrnes had moved to the telephone. "Dave," he said, "get me the Bomb Squad! Right away!"

"The Bom . . ."

"You heard me."

"Yes, *sir!*" Murchison said.

The call from the hospital came at 7:53, after the men from the Bomb Squad had gingerly removed the suspect bottle from the room. Byrnes took the call.

"Eighty-seventh Squad," he said. "Lieutenant Byrnes."

"This is Dr. Nelson at General. I was asked to call about the condition of this stabbing victim? José Dorena?"

"Yes," Byrnes said.

"He'll live. The blade missed the jugular by about a quarter of an inch. He won't be out of here for a while, but he'll be out alive." Nelson paused. "Anything else you want to know?"

"No. Thank you."

"Not at all," Nelson said, and he hung up.

Byrnes turned to Angelica, "You're lucky," he said. "Kassim'll live. You're a lucky girl."

And Angelica turned sad wise eyes toward the lieutenant and said, "Am I?"

Murchison walked over to her. "Come on, sweetie," he said, "we've got a room for you downstairs." He pulled her out of the chair, and then went to where Virginia Dodge was handcuffed to the radiator. "So you're the troublemaker, huh?" he said to her.

"Drop dead," Virginia told him.

"You got a key for this cuff, Pete?" Murchison said. He shook his head. "Jesus, Pete, why didn't you guys say something? I mean; I was sitting down there all this time. I mean . . ." He stopped as Byrnes handed him the key. "Hey, is that what you meant by 'Forthwith'?"

Byrnes nodded tiredly. "That is what I meant by 'Forthwith,'" he said.

"Yeah," Murchison said. "I'll be damned." Roughly, he pulled Virginia Dodge from the chair. "Come on, prize package," he said, and he led both women from the squadroom, passing Kling in the corridor.

"Well, we got Miscolo off okay," Kling said. "The rest is in the lap of the gods. We sent Meyer along for the ride. The intern seemed to think that face needed treatment. It's over, huh, Pete?"

"It's over," Byrnes said.

There was noise in the corridor outside. Steve Carella pushed Mark Scott through the slatted-rail divider and said, "Sit down, Scott. Over there. Hello, Pete. Cotton. Here's our boy. Strangled his own . . . Teddy! Honey, I forgot all about you. Have you been waiting lo— "

He shut his mouth because Teddy rushed into his arms with such fervor that she almost knocked him over.

"We've all been sort of waiting for you," Byrnes said.

"Yeah? Well, that's nice. Absence makes the heart grow fonder." He held Teddy at arm's length and said, "I'm sorry I'm late, baby. But all at once the thing began to jell and I . . ."

She touched the side of his neck where the blow from the rake had left marks crusted with blood.

"Oh, yeah," he said. "I got hit with a rake. Listen, let me type my report and away we go. Pete, I'm taking my wife to dinner, and I dare you to say no. We're going to have a baby!"

"Congratulations," Byrnes said wearily.

"Boy, what enthusiasm. Honey, let me type up this report, and away we go. I'm so starved I could eat a horse. Pete, we book this guy for homicide. Where's a typewriter? Anything interesting happen while I was . . . ?"

The phone rang.

"I've got it," Carella said. He lifted the receiver. "Eighty-seventh Squad, Carella."

"Carella, this is Levy down the Bomb Squad."

"Yeah, hi, Levy, how are you?"

"Fine. And you?"

"Fine. What's up?"

"I got a report on that bottle."

"What bottle?"

"We picked up a bottle there."

"Oh, yeah? Well, what about it?"

Carella listened, inserting a few "Uh-huhs" and "Yeses" into the conversation. Then he said, "Okay, Levy, thanks for the dope," and he hung up. He pulled up a chair, ripped three D.D. sheets from the desk drawer, inserted carbon between them, and then swung a typewriter into place.

"That was Levy," he said. "The Bomb Squad. Somebody here give him a bottle?"

"Yeah," Hawes said.

"Well, he was calling to report on it."

Hawes rose and walked to Carella "What did he say?"

"He said it was."

"It was?",

"That's what the man said. They exploded it downtown. Powerful enough to have blown up City Hall."

"It was," Hawes said tonelessly.

"Yeah." Carella inserted the report forms into the typewriter. "Was *what?*" he asked absently.

"Nitro," Hawes said, and he sank into a chair near the desk, and he had on his face the stunned expression of a man who's been hit by a Diesel locomotive.

"Boy," Carella said, "what a day *this* was!"

Furiously, he began typing.

The publishers hope that this large print book has brought you pleasurable reading. Each title is designed to make the text as easy to read as possible.

For further information on backlist or forthcoming titles please write or telephone:

In the British Isles and its territories, customers should contact:

ISIS Publishing Ltd
7 Centremead
Osney Mead
Oxford OX2 0ES
England
Telephone: (01865) 250 333 Fax: (01865) 790 358

In Australia and New Zealand, customers should contact:

Bolinda Publishing Pty Ltd
17 Mohr Street
Tullamarine Victoria 3043
Australia
Telephone: (03) 9338 0666 Fax: (03) 9335 1903
Toll Free Telephone: 1800 335 364
Toll Free Fax: 1800 671 4111

In New Zealand:
Toll Free Telephone: 0800 44 5788
Toll Free Fax: 0800 44 5789